Will
Irma
Taranee
Cornelia
Hay Lin
Part 1. The Twelve Portals
Volume 1

Part I. The Twelve Portals
Volume I

CONTENTS

1

Halloween

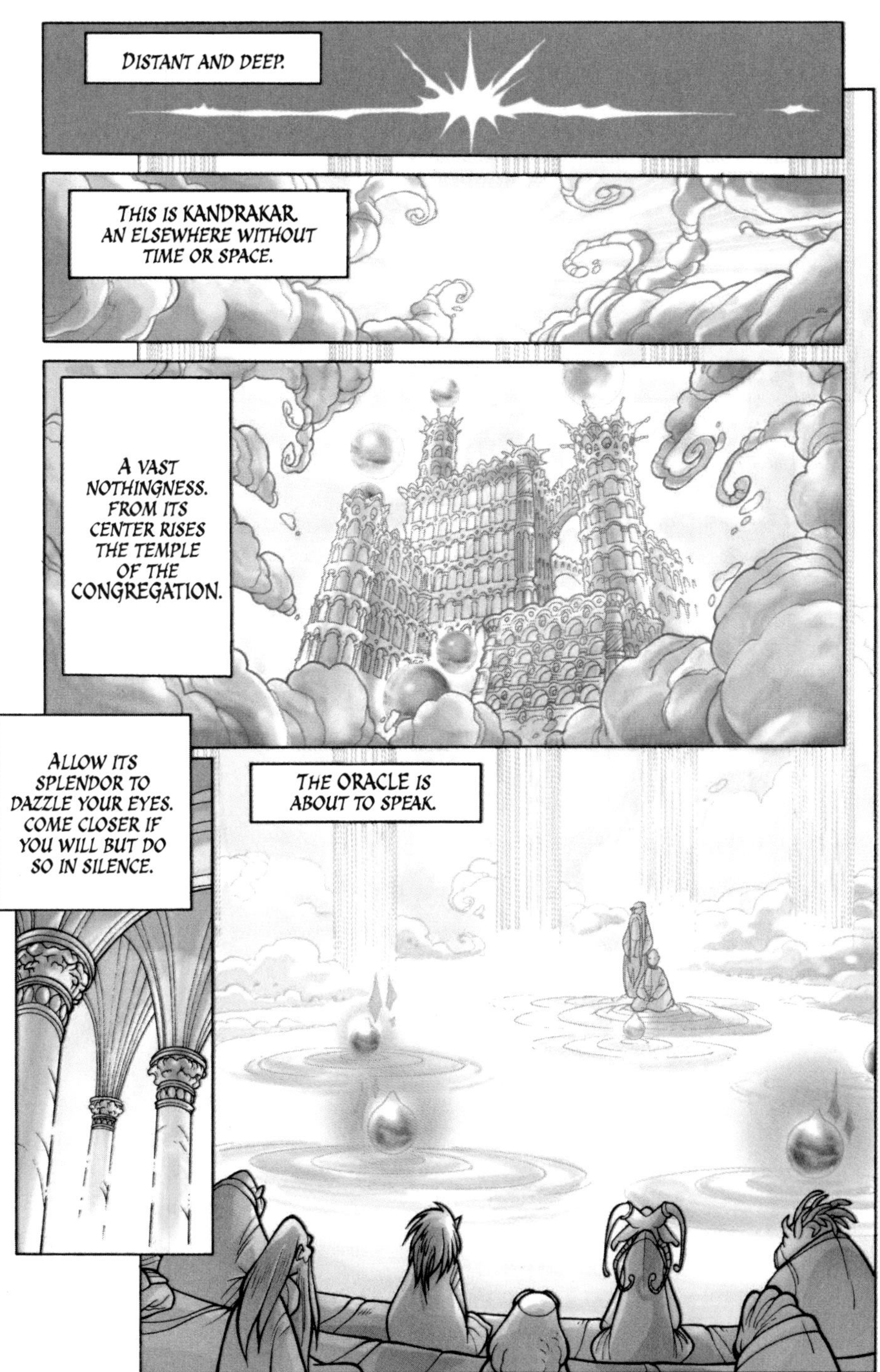
DISTANT AND DEEP.
THIS IS KANDRAKAR AN ELSEWHERE WITHOUT TIME OR SPACE.
A VAST NOTHINGNESS. FROM ITS CENTER RISES THE TEMPLE OF THE CONGREGATION.
ALLOW ITS SPLENDOR TO DAZZLE YOUR EYES. COME CLOSER IF YOU WILL BUT DO SO IN SILENCE.
THE ORACLE IS ABOUT TO SPEAK.

THERE IS NO MORE TIME, BROTHERS AND SISTERS! THE VEIL IS ONCE AGAIN IN DANGER.
IT IS TIME FOR GUARDIANS TO RETURN AND DEFEND THE ORDER OF ALL THINGS!
WHO WILL THE CHOSEN ONES BE THIS TIME, SIR?
FIVE GIRLS, ALTHOR.
HUMAN BEINGS?
MAGICAL BEINGS, LUBA. NATURE WILL BE THEIR FRIEND, THE EARTH, THEIR MOTHER, AND THE ELEMENTS, THEIR ALLIES.
AIR.
WATER.
EARTH.
FIRE.

AND THEN HER.
WILL.
WILL.
WILL.
WILL!

AH!
WAKE UP, WILL! DID YOU HAVE A BAD DREAM, HONEY?

SCARY! THERE WAS...THERE WAS A TERRIBLE STORM.
LOOKS LIKE IT'S RAINING CATS AND DOGS JUST ABOUT EVERYWHERE!

Waves of terrible weather continue to hit the entire country. On the coast...
CLICK

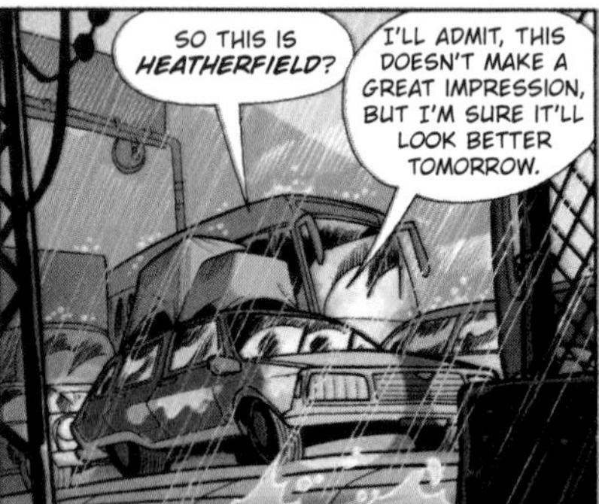

SO THIS IS HEATHERFIELD?
I'LL ADMIT, THIS DOESN'T MAKE A GREAT IMPRESSION, BUT I'M SURE IT'LL LOOK BETTER TOMORROW.

TOMORROW'S MY FIRST DAY OF SCHOOL, MOM.
SO THE DAY AFTER?

WELCOME TO HEATHERFIELD

2 M

60

"I KNEW SHE WOULD COME, VATHEK...

"SHE DETESTS THIS CITY, BUT SHE'LL SURVIVE..."

YES... I'M CERTAIN THAT THIS GIRL AND I SHALL GET ALONG WELL, OLD FRIEND!

9

IT WILL BE A PLEASURE TO DESTROY HER!

THE SUN SHINES ON A NEW DAY IN HEATHERFIELD. THE CLOUDS HAVE DISAPPEARED...

...FOR EVERYONE, EXCEPT ONE GIRL...

Sheffield Institute

STUPID ALARM! IF I'M SUPER-LATE, IT'S THAT ALARM'S FAULT! I CAN ALREADY HEAR MY TEACHER...

"OFF TO A BAD START, MISS VANDOM..."

NOW WHERE DO I GO?
WHAT DO I GOTTA DO TO GET TO CLASS 3A?
HOPE TO GET PROMOTED OUT OF 2A, MAYBE?
I HAD THAT SAME LOOK TWO DAYS AGO. I'M NEW HERE TOO. MY NAME'S TARANEE!
NICE TO MEET YOU. I'M WILL.
WOULD YOU PLEASE EXPLAIN WHY YOU'RE STILL IN THE HALL, LADIES?
IT'S THE PRINCIPAL! MS. KNICKER-BOCHER!
LESSONS HAVE ALREADY BEGUN, MISS COOK! STRAIGHT TO CLASS!
AS FOR YOU...
M-MY NAME'S WILL VANDOM, MA'AM, AND I THINK I'M A BIT LOST!
OFF TO A BAD START, MISS VANDOM...

BETTER LATE THAN NEVER, MISS COOK! STUDENTS ARE ALWAYS WELCOME HERE... ESPECIALLY WHEN THERE'S A *POP QUIZ*!

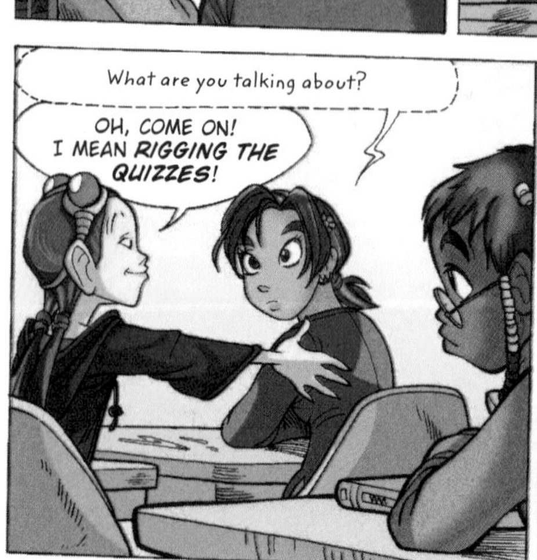

YEOW!
WHAT'S GOING ON BACK THERE?
GNAW

MR. COLLINS! HAY LIN BIT ME!
THAT'S A RAISED HAND! CONGRATULA-TIONS, IRMA! I NEEDED A VOLUNTEER, AND IT LOOKS LIKE I'VE FOUND ONE!

B-BUT THAT'S NOT FAIR!
Watch and learn, Taranee! When Irma's quizzed, first she gets angry, then she gets desperate...

Shut up! I didn't study at all! All I know is a little about Charles the Great...
...THEN SHE SHUTS HER EYES TIGHT, CLASPS HER HANDS...

AskmeaboutCharlestheGreat! Pleaseohpleaseohplease...
...AND IF THERE'S ONLY ONE THING SHE STUDIED, THAT'S WHAT THEY'RE GONNA ASK HER ABOUT! I DON'T KNOW HOW SHE DOES IT! ALL I KNOW FOR SURE...

"...IS IT WORKS EVERY TIME!"
HMMM... LET'S SEE HERE...
HISTO

IRMA LAIR... WHY DON'T YOU TELL US ABOUT CHARLES THE GREAT?
YUS!

DRIIIIIIING

2 B
HA! I CAN'T BELIEVE IT! YOU DID IT AGAIN!
HEY! IT'S A SECRET! YOU CAN'T GO TELLING THE WHOLE SCHOOL!

WHAT CAN'T SHE TELL US?
CORNELIA! THE REMOTE-CONTROLLED QUIZZES! SHE DID IT AGAIN!
CONTROLLING QUIZZES! SHE THINKS SHE'S A BIG SHOT, BUT SHE'S JUST A BEGINNER!

IF SHE ONLY KNEW WHAT I CAN DO...
SEE YOU TOMORROW!
WHO WAS THAT?
TARANEE, ONE OF THE NEW GIRLS. THE OTHER ONE'S IN CLASS WITH YOU AND ELYON, RIGHT?

YEAH, I THINK HER NAME'S WILL. ASK ELYON. SHE ALWAYS HAS THE DIRT!
HI, GUYS...

HOLD UP, ELYON. I'VE SEEN THIS FACE BEFORE!

ME TOO—IN A DOCUMENTARY ABOUT EASTER ISLAND...

OH, NO, NO, NO, CORNELIA! I KNOW "***FLUNKED***" WHEN I SEE IT...

...AND I'D SAY WHAT WE HAVE HERE IS A BIG, FAT, HAIRY "F"!

ALL RIGHT, ALREADY! I GOT A BAD GRADE IN MATH! SATISFIED?

OF COURSE I AM! 'COS YOU KNOW WHAT THAT MEANS, RIGHT?

PUUUUNISHMENT!

AWW, COME ON... COULDN'T YOU LET IT GO JUST ONCE...?

YOU KNOW THE RULES!

FOR A PARTICULARLY BAD GRADE, WE NEED SOMETHING PARTICULARLY NASTY!
IT'S STRANGE, THOUGH. I THOUGHT MATT-EMATICS WAS YOUR FAVORITE SUBJECT...
LEAVE MATT OUT OF THIS!
OF COURSE! HE'LL BE YOUR PUNISHMENT! YOU'LL GET YOUR DREAM BOY TO HELP YOU STUDY!
YOU GOTTA CONVINCE HIM! BEGGING AND PLEADING!
IT'S ONE OR THE OTHER, IRMA. EITHER SHE BEGS OR SHE PLEADS!
I VOTE BEGS! IT WAS MY IDEA ANYWAY!
WHAT IF WE MAKE HER BEG PLEADINGLY?
THAT'S LAME!
BUT IT'S A COMPROMISE!
GOOD LUCK, ELYON!

WHAT'S GOING ON OVER THERE?
DID YOU GUYS DO THIS?
HEH-HEH-HEH! COULD BE!
HAH! LOOKS LIKE SOMEBODY'S GONNA BE WALKIN' HOME TODAY!

YOU GUYS ARE NEW, AIN'TCHA? YOU'RE CUTE!

AND YOU'RE THE SAME OLD MORON, ***URIAH***...

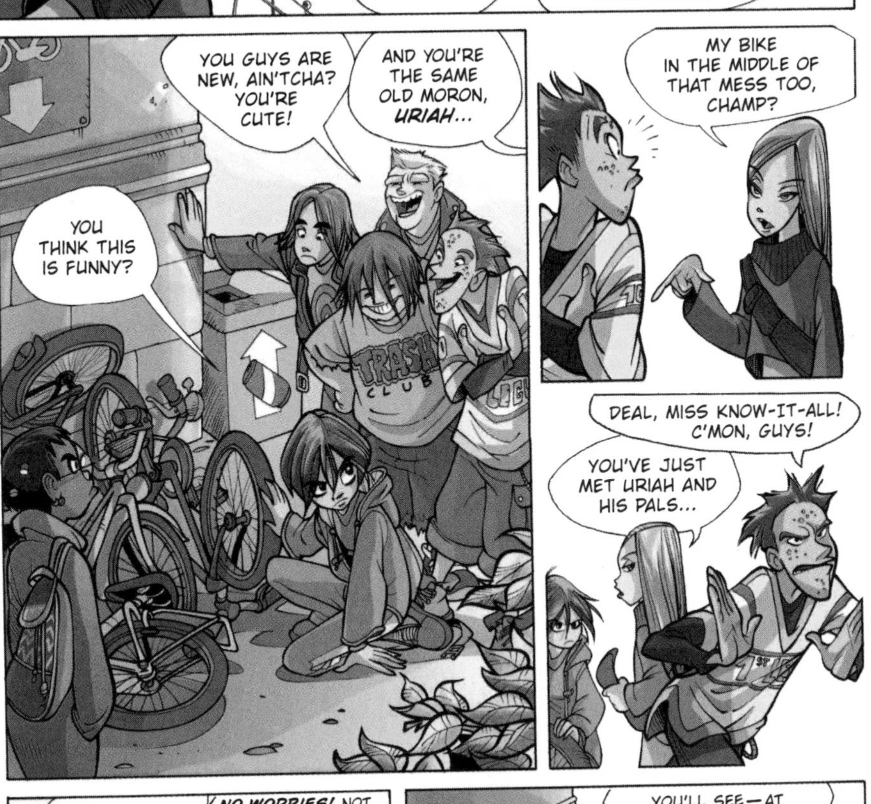

YOU THINK THIS IS FUNNY?

MY BIKE IN THE MIDDLE OF THAT MESS TOO, CHAMP?

DEAL, MISS KNOW-IT-ALL! C'MON, GUYS!

YOU'VE JUST MET URIAH AND HIS PALS...

I COULD'VE DONE WITHOUT!
NO WORRIES! NOT EVERYONE IN THE FOURTH CLASS IS LIKE THAT.

YOU'LL SEE—AT TONIGHT'S PARTY!
OH NO... THE PARTY! I TOTALLY FORGOT!

TARANEE, RIGHT? I'M CORNELIA!
NICE TO MEET YOU!
KRUNKL

WE'RE ALL MEETING AT THE GYM AT EIGHT O'CLOCK. YOU'LL SEE! IT'LL BE A PARTY ***TO REMEMBER***!
CLANK

AS FAR AS I'M CONCERNED, I JUST WANT TO FORGET TODAY AS SOON AS POSSIBLE!

AND MAKE SURE YOU WEAR SOMETHING ***FRIGHTENINGLY SPECIAL***!
I'LL SEE WHAT I CAN DO!

SEE YA LATER, THEN!
I DON'T KNOW, CORNELIA... I HAVEN'T BEEN TO A PARTY IN AGES...

THEN THIS'LL BE YOUR CHANCE TO GET BACK INTO THE HABIT! ***BYE!***

-GRUNT- SHOW'S OVER...
THE SHOW AIN'T EVEN STARTED, GUYS!
-YAWN-
Sheffield Institute

COME WITH ME!

THE COAST IS CLEAR, URIAH!
KEEP A LOOKOUT...

SEE THESE? I TOOK 'EM FROM MY OLD MAN'S BOAT...
THOSE ARE FLARES! WHADDAYA GONNA DO WITH 'EM?

THE SCHOOL MAY BE TAKIN' CARE OF THE MUSIC AND THE EATS AT TONIGHT'S PARTY...

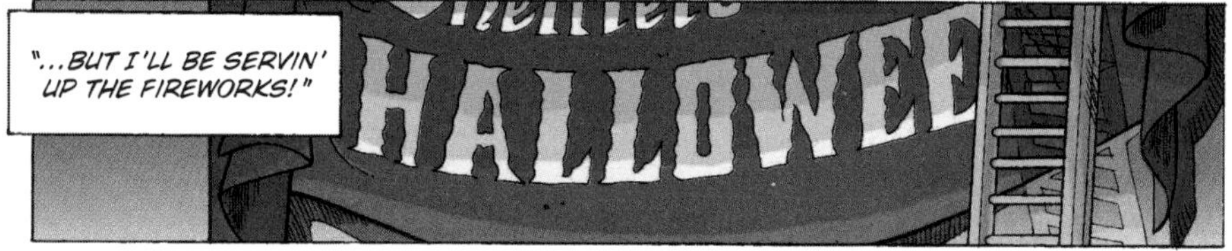
"...BUT I'LL BE SERVIN' UP THE FIREWORKS!"
HALLOWEE

I'M NOT REALLY UP TO GOING TO THE PARTY... I'M TIRED, AND I MIGHT HAVE TO HELP MY MOM SET UP HER INTERNET CONNECTION.
WELL, IF YOU'RE NOT GOING, I'M NOT EITHER!

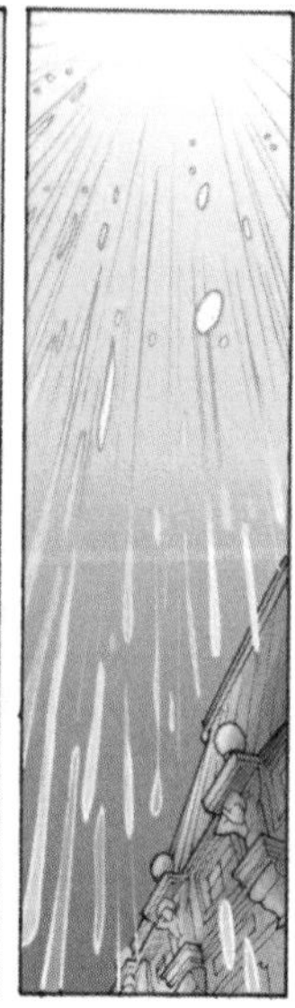

MEANWHILE...
...NO, IRMA, I HAVEN'T DECIDED WHAT I'M WEARING YET, BUT IT'S TOTALLY GONNA BE SOMETHING SPECTACULAR!
THE SILVER DRAGON
CHINESE RESTAURANT

ALL I CAN SAY IS I DESIGNED IT MYSELF, AND WHEN I WALK IN, EVERYBODY'S HEAD'S GONNA TURN!
PRINCESS SUSHI

OF COURSE IT'LL BE READY BY EIGHT! ***YOU'LL SEE...***

IT'LL BE SOMETHING UNIQUE! EXTRAORDINARY! SOMETHING... SOMETHING ***BEWITCHING***!
!
KLICKITI

WITH A COUPLE STITCHES, IT'LL BE READY IN TEN MINUTES!
RIGHT, GRANDMA?
TEN MINUTES, AS ALWAYS!

I'M REALLY CURIOUS! HAY LIN'S ALWAYS GOT A TON OF IDEAS!

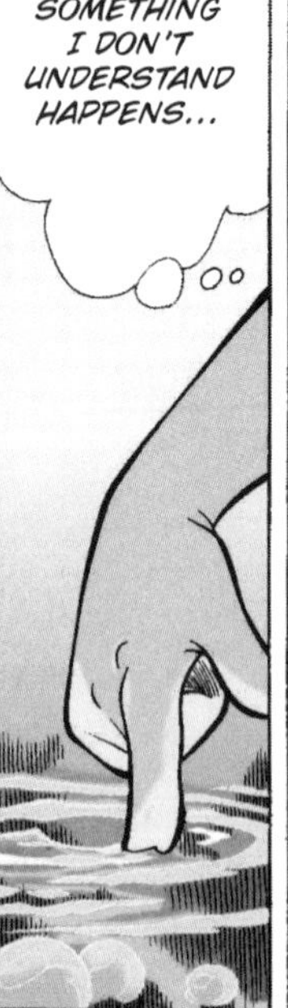

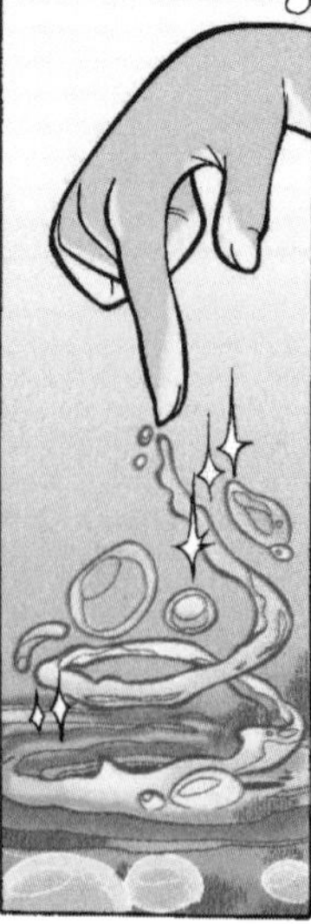

...MAGICAL!

IRMA!
SPLASH
PLOSH

ARE YOU DONE? YOU'VE BEEN IN THERE FOR OVER AN HOUR!
JUST A SEC!

COME ON, EVAPORATE! I DON'T WANT DAD TO SEE THIS MESS!

IRMA? I'M WARNING YOU, I'M LOSING MY PATIENCE!
I-I'M COMING!

IRMA!
COMING!
SVLAP
SVLAP

NEXT TIME, I'M BUSTING DOWN THE DOOR! YOU KNOW I CAN!
OH, YEAH? ON WHOSE AUTHORITY?

A TWO-HOUR BATH ISN'T A CRIME!

IF YOU GOT PRUNY FINGERS LIKE ALL NORMAL PEOPLE, YOU WOULDN'T ACT LIKE THIS...

BUT NO! THE LITTLE LADY CAN STAY IN THERE, SOAKING ALL AFTERNOON LIKE IT WAS NOTHING! GOOD GRIEF!
I KNOW MY RIGHTS, OFFICER, SIR!

IRMA! THERE'S A LAKE IN HERE!
I'LL ONLY SPEAK IN THE PRESENCE OF MY ATTORNEY!

PHEW! IT'S TOUGH BEING THIRTEEN!
SLAM

I ENVY YOU, LEAFY! I'D LOVE A NICE SHELL LIKE YOURS...THE SAME OUTFIT EVERY DAY, YOUR WHOLE LIFE...
?

...BUT I, ON THE OTHER HAND, HAVE TO CHOOSE, DARN IT! WHY CAN'T I EVER FIND WHAT I WANT?

A NICE DARK-BLUE DRESS! IS THAT TOO MUCH TO ASK? ONE SIMPLE WISH...
KARMILLA

HUH?

!

GULP!

IT STOPPED RAINING! I BETTER GO!

THANKS FOR HAVING ME OVER, TARANEE!

WHICH LOOK ARE YOU GOING FOR TONIGHT? SCARY OR ELEGANT?

I ALWAYS LOOK SCARY! I'VE DECIDED TO TRY SOMETHING NEW...

HA-HA-HA!

26

MAYBE I SPOKE TOO SOON...AN ELEGANT DRESS MIGHT NOT HAVE BEEN SUCH A BRIGHT IDEA!

I'D FEEL A LOT BETTER WEARING A **SWEAT SUIT**!
I SHOULD ASK AROUND! MAYBE THEY SELL **EVENING SWEATS** SOMEWHERE!

IF THEY DO EXIST, I BET THEY ALL HAVE **RHINESTONE** ZIPPERS!
Ye Olde B

HUH?

SKREEE..

YE OLDE BOOK SHOP

Ye olde Bookshop

IT...
IT CAN'T BE...

ANOTHER HOUSE,
ANOTHER ARGUMENT...

FORGET IT, YOUNG LADY! YOU'RE GOING NOWHERE TONIGHT!
AT LEAST NOT UNTIL YOU'VE CLEANED YOUR ROOM!
C'MON, MOM! I'LL DO IT TOMORROW!

AND WHAT'S STOPPING YOU FROM DOING IT NOW?
GENETICS! I'M NATURALLY AVERSE TO BLACKMAIL!

WHATEVER, CORNELIA! IF THIS IS A SHOWDOWN, YOU'RE THE ONE WITH SOMETHING TO LOSE!

NEAT! LOOKS LIKE WE'LL ALL BE HOME TOGETHER TONIGHT, HUH?
SHUT IT, YOU LITTLE TOAD!

CROAK
DANG IT! WHY CAN'T ROOMS JUST CLEAN THEMSELVES?

HUH?
SLAM

CLACK
CLACK
CLACK

CLACK
CLACK

CLACK
CLACK
CLACK

HNF
STUPID DOOR!
WHY WON'T IT...?

WOW!

I...
I CAN'T BELIEVE IT! JUST A THOUGHT MADE IT HAPPEN!

WHAT IRMA CAN DO IN CLASS IS NOTHING COMPARED TO WHAT I'VE BEEN ABLE TO DO LATELY!

AT SCHOOL, I CONTROL EVERYTHING JUST BY WISHING FOR IT!
...AND NOW THIS...

WHAT'S HAPPENING TO ME?
CORNELIA! WHERE DO YOU THINK YOU'RE GOING?
TO THE PARTY! MY ROOM'S CLEAN!

CORNELIA? FOR YOUR SAKE, THAT BETTER BE TRUE! CORNELIA!
HEY! DID I MISS SOMETHING?
BYE, POP!

THE SHEFFIELD INSTITUTE GYMNASIUM, 8:00 P.M.
GREAT PARTY...
Sheffield Institute's HALLOWEEN
...AND A GREAT DRESS, HAY LIN!
THANK YOU, MA'AM! YOURS ISN'T TOO SHABBY EITHER!
SHE JUST THREW ON THE FIRST THING SHE SAW!
BON APPÉTIT! FROM THE LOOKS OF YOUR ***BOOTY***, I'D SAY YOU ALL LIKE THE BUFFET!
IT'S NOT HOW IT LOOKS, MS. KNICKERBOCHER! WE'RE JUST STOCKIN' UP FOR ***WINTER***!
SO ANOTHER SCHOOL YEAR WASTED ***HIBERNATING***... EXCELLENT!
WITCH! *YOU WON'T BE LAUGHIN' COME MIDNIGHT!*
AT ELEVEN...
WILL! IT'S SUPER-LATE! AND WE STILL HAVE TO PICK UP YOUR FRIEND!

WHO CARES ABOUT THE PARTY? I DIDN'T WANNA GO ANY-WAY! YOU'RE THE ONE WHO INSISTED!
PLUS, I HAVE NOTHING TO WEAR! EVERYTHING I PUT ON MAKES ME LOOK LIKE A SURFBOARD, AND...
...AND...
THIS... THIS ISN'T ME!
WILL?
AHHH! DON'T COME IN! DON'T COME IN!

?

WHY AREN'T YOU DRESSED YET? AREN'T YOU WEARING THE BLACK ONE? IT USED TO BE YOUR FAVORITE!
THE ONLY THING BLACK THAT'D LOOK GOOD ON ME IS A *GARBAGE BAG*!

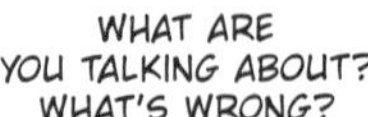
WHAT ARE YOU TALKING ABOUT? WHAT'S WRONG?

I LOOK LIKE... NO...I AM A BROOMSTICK!

YOU'RE A VERY SPECIAL PERSON WHO'S GOING TO MEET VERY SPECIAL FRIENDS AT THE PARTY!

LOOK AT YOURSELF, WILL! YOU HAVE TO LOVE YOURSELF. THAT'S THE ONLY WAY PEOPLE CAN APPRECIATE HOW SPECIAL YOU ARE!

"NOW, LET'S GET GOING! THE PARTY WON'T LAST FOREVER!"
HAVE A GREAT TIME! HEY, TARANEE, TAKE GOOD CARE OF WILL FOR ME!
SEE YA LATER!
PARTY
MY LITTLE GIRL'S A BIT SHY. PUT A LITTLE FIRE INTO HER!
I DON'T KNOW IF I'M THE RIGHT PERSON FOR THE JOB, BUT I'LL TRY!

THERE'S STILL TIME, TARANEE! LET'S TURN AROUND AND GET OUTTA HERE!
LOOKS LIKE IT'S TOO LATE!
PARTY
HEY THERE, GUYS!

A COUPLE HOURS LATE— "FASHIONABLY LATE," YOU MIGHT SAY...
CORNELIA!

IT'S MY FAULT! I LOST TRACK OF TIME, AND...
HEAR THAT, IRMA? THAT'S WHAT I CALL AN ORIGINAL EXCUSE!

SHE SHOWED UP LATE TOO. WANNA HEAR THE EXCUSE SHE CAME UP WITH?
IT'S NOT FUNNY! ALL MY CLOTHES TRANSFORMED AND CHANGED COLOR!

AH AH AH AH AH AH AH
IT'S THE TRUTH! IF YOU DON'T BELIEVE ME, THAT'S YOUR PROBLEM!
I BELIEVE YOU!

HOW ABOUT A PICTURE, PRETTY LADIES?
SURE! SMILE, GUYS!
I'M NEVER TELLING YOU ANYTHING EVER AGAIN, SO THERE!

KANDRAKAR

THE NEW **GUARDIANS,** TIBOR! LOOK AT THEM!

THEY ARE CLOSE...
...BUT NOT YET UNITED.

YOU WON'T HAVE TO WAIT LONG FOR THAT. SOON, THE SECRET WILL BE REVEALED, AND THE FIVE WILL BE ONE AT LAST!

FIVE? I SEE ***SIX*** OF THEM, SIR!

ONE WILL ***BETRAY*** THE OTHERS, MY FRIEND...

"THE MOMENT OF ALLIANCE WILL ALSO BE THE MOMENT OF DECEPTION!"

THIRTY MINUTES TILL MIDNIGHT, MY FRIENDS! HALLOWEEN IS HERE! ***A BIG SHOUT OUT TO THE GREAT PUMPKIN! YEAAAH!***

CUTE, HUH? THAT'S ***MATT***, THE BOY ELYON LIKES. HE'S IN THE FOURTH CLASS.

SO NOT EVERYBODY IN FOURTH'S LIKE URIAH, HUH...

EXIT
HEY! WHAT DO YOU THINK ABOUT THAT GUY WHO JUST WALKED IN?
NEVER SEEN HIM BEFORE! HE LOOKS OUT OF THIS WORLD!
HOW CAN YOU TELL WITH THE MASK?
HE STILL LOOKS OUT OF THIS WORLD!
THEY ALL SEEM OUT OF THIS WORLD TO YOU, HAY LIN!
THAT'S NOT TRUE! FOR EXAMPLE, THE ONE WALKING UP TO YOU NOW IS UUUGLY!
HOW ABOUT ANOTHER PICTURE, SWEET THING? JUST YOU AND ME?
DISAPPEAR, MARTIN!
YOU KNOW SOMETHING, GIRLS? I'D SAY THAT GUY OVER THERE IS CUTE ENOUGH FOR ELYON'S PUNISHMENT!
BET HE GIVES GREAT MATH LESSONS!
SHE'S COMING TOWARD US, SIR!
I'LL TAKE CARE OF HER, VATHEK! YOU FOCUS ON THE REDHEAD. YOU KNOW WHAT TO DO...
YOU CAN COUNT ON ME, SIR! IN ALL THIS CONFUSION, NO ONE WILL NOTICE ME!

WE'RE TAKING BETS ON ELYON, LADIES! I SAY SHE WON'T DO IT!
WELL... SHE DID LOOK PRETTY DETERMINED!

WHAT DO YOU THINK, WILL?
I...I...

HEY!
MAKE WAY! FOOD COMING THROUGH!
...I SAY ELYON CAN DO IT...

CURSE YOU! I ALMOST HAD HER...

EVERY-THING OKAY?
I GUESS SO... DO YOU GUYS HEAR THAT STRANGE HUMMING?
THE MUSIC'S TOO LOUD! LET'S MOVE!

UM...H-HI!
HELLO, ELYON...
YOU... YOU KNOW MY NAME? WHO ARE YOU?
MY NAME'S **CEDRIC**, BABE...
...AND I KNOW A LOT ABOUT YOU!
UNNH...
WILL! DO YOU FEEL OKAY?
JUST A DIZZY SPELL, TARANEE. SOME FRESH AIR MIGHT HELP.
WE'LL GO WITH!
NOW WHERE ARE THEY GOING? CAN'T LOSE SIGHT OF THEM!
HEY! COOL COSTUME, BUD!
GET OUT OF MY WAY, MISERABLE CREATURE!
KRUMP
OW! WATCH WHERE YOU'RE GOING, YOU BIG OX!
HUMANS! THEY WOULDN'T BE SO FRIENDLY IF THEY KNEW THIS IS HOW I TRULY LOOK!

WHO... WHO SAID THAT?
I DID!
BY THE MOONS OF GAAHN! AN INVISIBLE BEING!
HEY, I MAY NOT BE VERY POPULAR, BUT YOU DON'T GOTTA RUB MY NOSE IN IT!

ANYWAY, GREAT MASK! YOU DESERVE A PHOTO!
WAMP
ARGH!

MY EYES! AAAARRRGGGHHH! I CAN'T STAND LIGHT!
PFFFF
PFFF

GRRRRHAAARRR!
CRANKLE
HEY!
HUH?
SCRASH

CAME OUT A BIT BLURRY, I'D SAY...
YOUR ATTENTION FOR A MOMENT, PLEASE! ONLY THREE MINUTES LEFT UNTIL MIDNIGHT...
YOU'LL PAY FOR THIS, MICROBE!

...SO NOW IT'S TIME TO BURN OUR JACK-O'-LANTERN! BUT FIRST, WE'LL AWARD THE PRIZE FOR BEST COSTUME OF THE EVENING!

LET'S SEE...I COULD TURN YOU INTO A WART, BUT I'M NOT SURE ANYONE WOULD NOTICE THE *DIFFERENCE*!
...AND BY UNANIMOUS VOTE, ***LADIES AND GENTLEMEN...***

...THE WINNER!
WHA...? DO THEY MEAN ME?
I'M AFRAID NOT...

NOW WHAT HAPPENS?
IT'S THE GRAND FINALE! THE PERSON WITH THE BEST COSTUME GETS THE HONOR OF SETTING THE JACK-O'-LANTERN ON ***FIRE!***
YEEAAH!
YA-HOO!

LET ME GO! RELEASE ME! YOU'RE MAKING A BIG MISTAKE! YOU'LL BE SORRY FOR THIS!
HALLOWEEN! HALLOWEEN!
HALLOWEEN!
HALLOWEEN!

BE A SPORT, YOUNG MAN! BEFORE WE FIND OUT WHO'S BENEATH THIS OUTSTANDING MASK, SHALL WE GET OUR BONFIRE GOING?

NO ONE TREATS VATHEK IN THIS MANNER! YOU HAVE GONE TOO FAR, YOU REPULSIVE MASS OF CELLS!
I RECOGNIZE YOU! YOU'RE SAMSON FROM CLASS 4B, AREN'T YOU? WELL, I DON'T FIND YOU THE LEAST BIT AMUSING!

HERE WE GO, URIAH!
PUTTIN' THOSE FLARES IN THE PUMPKIN WASN'T SUCH A GOOD IDEA!
TOO LATE NOW, NIGEL! JUST RELAX AND ENJOY THE SHOW!

"...'COS I THINK IT'S GONNA BE DYNAMITE!"
UM, I'M SAMSON, MA'AM.
HUH? THEN WHO ARE YOU?

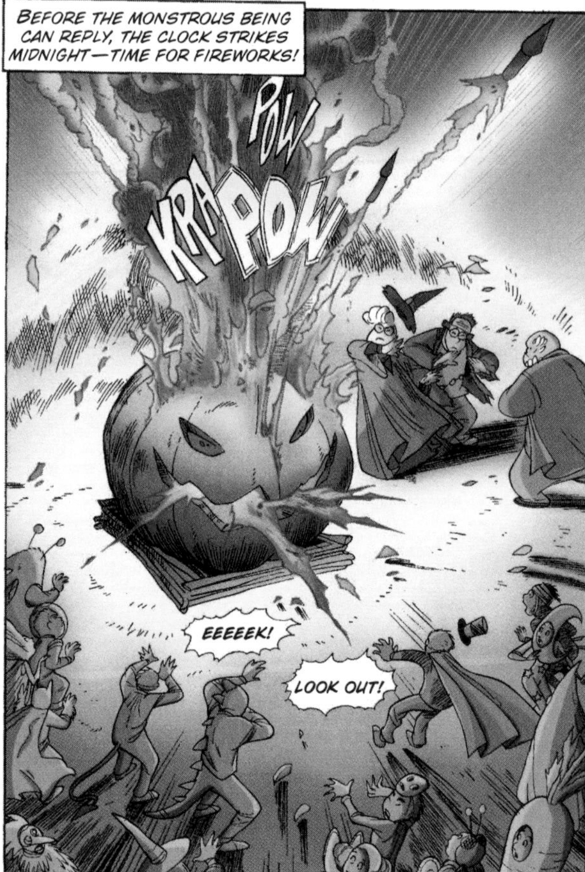
BEFORE THE MONSTROUS BEING CAN REPLY, THE CLOCK STRIKES MIDNIGHT—TIME FOR FIREWORKS!
POW!
KRAPOW!
EEEEEK!
LOOK OUT!

HA-HA-HA!
LOOK AT 'EM RUN!
WOW!
EVERYTHING'S ON FIRE, URIAH! THIS WASN'T SUPPOSED TO HAPPEN!

THE GIRL! I CAN'T LET THIS CHANCE PASS ME BY!
LET'S GET OUT OF HERE! QUICK!

YEOW!
POW

IRMA, DUCK!
EEEEK!

STOP!

FZZZKZZKZ

FWEEEOOOOOoo..
WITH A WAVE OF TARANEE'S HAND, THE ROCKET SUDDENLY CHANGES COURSE...

FWEEOOOOOoo

...WITH UNEXPECTED RESULTS!
BWOOOOM
AAAH!

WILL!

FWOOOOOOSH
BACK!

WHAT'S GOING ON, TARANEE? HOW... HOW'D YOU DO THAT?
I DON'T KNOW, WILL!

I REALLY DON'T KNOW...

45

"THE PARTY IS OVER, LORD CEDRIC."

YOU'RE MISTAKEN, VATHEK. THE PARTY HAS NOT YET BEGUN!

"AND TOMORROW COMES THE GRAND FINALE!"
IT WAS INCREDIBLE! IT WAS ALL SO REAL! I DON'T KNOW HOW TO DESCRIBE IT...
THAT PLACE... THOSE CREATURES... THE SOUNDS... THE NOISES... EVEN THE SMELLS... IT WAS LIKE I WAS REALLY THERE!
AND IT WAS TERRIFYING—UNTIL THAT PENDANT APPEARED!
THEN WHAT HAPPENED?
MY ALARM CLOCK WENT OFF!
HALLOWEEN WAS OVER, BUT IT LEFT SOMETHING IN ITS WAKE...
...SOMETHING THAT WOULD CHANGE THE LIVES OF THESE GIRLS...
...FOREVER!
DID THE PENDANT LOOK SOMETHING LIKE THIS?

GOSH, *YEAH*!
HANG ON A SECOND! THAT'S THE SAME THING I DREAMED ABOUT!

YOU TOO?
IRMA *NEVER* DESCRIBED IT, AND NEITHER DID I! HOW'D YOU *KNOW*?
SIMPLE...

...I SAW IT IN MY DREAM TOO!
STOP! JUST STOP IT!

THIS STUFF... THIS STUFF IS *SCARING* ME! WHAT'S GOING ON?
LET'S THINK IT THROUGH. STRANGE THINGS HAVE HAPPENED TO JUST ABOUT ALL OF US...
CLEAN

...UNEXPLAINABLE THINGS WE'RE DEFINITELY NOT JUST *IMAGINING*!
...SO, SHERLOCK?

SO NOTHING! MAYBE WE ALL NEED TO TALK IT OVER CALMLY! BUT *NOT HERE* AND *NOT NOW*!
CORNELIA'S RIGHT! COME OVER TO MY HOUSE THIS AFTERNOON!

FINE BY ME!
SAME HERE! IT'S SETTLED, THEN!

I...I DON'T KNOW IF I CAN MAKE IT...
GOT SOMETHING BETTER TO DO, ELLIE?

I'VE GOT A DATE WITH CEDRIC! THAT GUY FROM LAST NIGHT, REMEMBER?
YOU DON'T SAY! DID YOU CONVINCE HIM TO STUDY WITH YOU, ELYON?

HE'S SO FASCINATING! HE INVITED ME TO HIS BOOKSTORE! HE SAYS HE HAS TO TALK TO ME!
A LITTLE CHAT IN A BOOKSTORE? JUST THINKING ABOUT IT MAKES ME YAWN!

YOU'RE JEALOUS!
IS IT THAT OBVIOUS?
HA-HA-HA! WELL, HAVE FUN, ELYON!

"WE'D BE THE LAST ONES TO TRY AND STOP YOU!"
FOUR O'CLOCK SHARP! YOU CAN DO THIS! JUST TAKE A DEEP BREATH AND...
Book-Shop

TL'NG
UM... HELLO? ANYBODY HERE?
I'M RIGHT HERE, ELYON!

...I'VE BEEN WAITING FOR YOU!
!

MEANWHILE, AT HAY LIN'S HOUSE...
...SO HOW DO YOU EXPLAIN ALL THIS?

WELL, IT'S NOT LIKE THERE HAS TO BE AN EXPLANATION, CORNELIA!
NO! EVERYTHING HAPPENS FOR A REASON, AND I WANT TO KNOW WHAT'S GOING ON!

AS FAR AS I'M CONCERNED, I WANT YOU ALL TO KNOW I DON'T BELIEVE IN MAGIC OR PARANORMAL PHENOMENA!
MYSTERIOUS DREAMS, CLOTHES CHANGING COLOR, FLAMES FOLLOWING COMMANDS, PREMONITIONS! WHAT DO YOU CALL ALL THAT?

CHOMP
GROWING PAINS?

MAYBE THE PENDANT'S GOT THE ANSWERS WE'RE LOOKING FOR...
LOOK AT THIS! I SKETCHED A BETTER COPY!

...HOPE I DIDN'T FORGET ANYTHING!
I'D SAY IT'S ALL THERE!
HMM...YUP, SURE LOOKS LIKE IT...

...BUT PERHAPS THIS LOOKS EVEN MORE LIKE IT?

GRANDMA!
THAT'S IT! WHERE'D YOU GET THAT?

WHAT'S IMPORTANT IS THAT YOU'LL BE KEEPING IT NOW! THIS IS THE HEART OF KANDRAKAR!

...AND YOU ARE THE NEW GUARDIANS!
WH-WHAT ARE YOU TALKING ABOUT?

LET ME TELL YOU A STORY, GIRLS! A STORY AS OLD AS TIME...

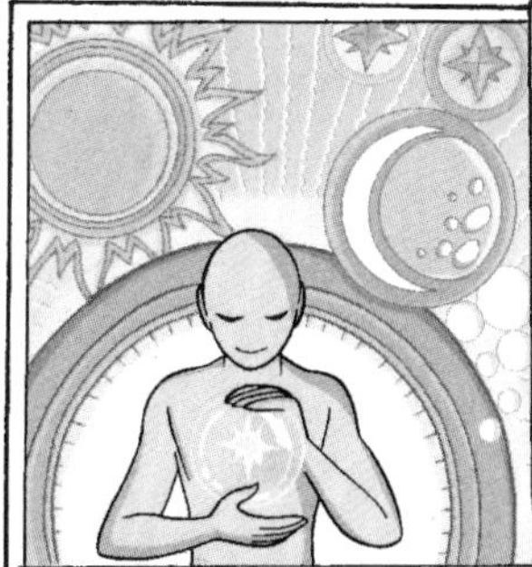
...A DISTANT TIME WHEN EVERYTHING WAS YOUNG AND SPIRITS AND CREATURES LIVED UNDER THE SAME SKY!

THERE WAS A SINGLE UNIVERSE, AN IMMENSE KINGDOM RULED BY NATURE... A KINGDOM THAT LASTED EONS...

...UNTIL SPIRITS AND CREATURES LEARNED EVIL AND ALL WAS DIVIDED INTO THOSE WHO WANTED PEACE AND THOSE WHO THRIVED ON OTHERS' PAIN.

TO SEPARATE THE TWO SIDES, THE *VEIL* WAS CREATED. EVIL AND INJUSTICE WERE BANISHED TO THE DARK REALM CALLED ***METAMOOR***.
BEFORE SEPARATING FOR ETERNITY, THE UNIVERSE GAVE LIFE TO THE FORTRESS OF KANDRAKAR, IN THE VERY HEART OF INFINITY.

THERE, THE MIGHTIEST SPIRITS AND CREATURES STAND GUARD...

THERE, THE PROTECTORS OF THE *VEIL* RESIDE. AND THERE, IF YOU WISH, YOU MAY ALSO JOURNEY...

IT IS NO COINCIDENCE THAT YOU ARE ALL HERE. YOU ARE THE NEW GUARDIANS OF THE VEIL—THE MOST IMPORTANT WARRIORS IN A BATTLE THAT BEGAN THOUSANDS OF YEARS AGO!
THE VEIL?
THE WORLD IS ACTUALLY MADE UP OF MANY DIFFERENT WORLDS, AND THE VEIL IS THE VERY FABRIC THAT DIVIDES THEM...
...A MESH WHOSE FIBERS HAVE BECOME DANGEROUSLY FRAGILE!
I... I'M AFRAID I DON'T UNDERSTAND.
TO UNDERSTAND, LISTEN TO YOUR TWO HEARTS. ONE BEATS WITHIN YOU...
...AND THE OTHER IS THE HEART OF KANDRAKAR! THE FORCES OF NATURE LIE WITHIN, AND NOW AND FOREVERMORE, THEY WILL BE WITH YOU!
YOU, IRMA, WILL HAVE POWER OVER WATER, UNBROKEN AND UNCONTAINABLE...

TO YOU, FIRM CORNELIA, THE POWER OF *EARTH*.

GENEROUS TARANEE, YOURS IS THE DIFFICULT GIFT OF *FIRE*.

AND YOU, MY LITTLE HAY LIN, WILL BE FREE AND LIGHT AS THE *AIR*!

AND ME?

GIVE ME YOUR HAND, WILL!

YOU WILL FIND OUT SOON ENOUGH!

AH!
THIS... THIS IS MAGIC!

WE WILL MEET AGAIN SOON!
HANG ON! **WAIT!** DON'T...

...LEAVE!

HERE THEY ARE, ORACLE! NOW THEY ARE TOGETHER!
OUR WAITING IS OVER!

THE CONGREGATION IS GRATEFUL TO YOU, HONORABLE YAN LIN. YOUR TASK HAS BEEN COMPLETED. THE TIME HAS COME...
WE CAN BEGIN!

I DON'T REALLY GET WHAT JUST HAPPENED!
NOTHING! WITH ALL DUE RESPECT, HAY LIN, I THINK YOUR GRANDMA HAS A FEW SCREWS LOOSE!

SHE TOLD US THAT RIDICULOUS STORY HOPING SHE'D AMAZE US BY USING THAT **TRICK** WITH THE SHINING PENDANT!
YOU'RE **AFRAID**, AREN'T YOU, CORNELIA?

I DON'T BELIEVE IN FAIRY TALES, IRMA! THIS IS DIFFERENT—AND NOW I'M GOING HOME!
I KNOW HER. SHE'LL CHANGE HER MIND...
OPEN

IF WE'RE SOME KINDA SUPERGROUP, WE SHOULD HAVE COSTUMES, DON'CHA THINK?
AND A NAME! WHAT DO YOU THINK ABOUT "*WITCH*"?

IT'S OUR INITIALS PUT TOGETHER! *W-I-T-C-H!* ISN'T THAT CUTE?
ALL THAT INK IS GOING TO END UP POISONING YOU, HAY LIN!
IT'S ALREADY POISONED HER! WITCH! I'VE NEVER HEARD ANYTHING SO DUMB!
WITCH

I DON'T FEEL LIKE A WITCH! HOW ABOUT YOU, WILL?
I...I DON'T KNOW! I'M STILL KINDA CONFUSED! I DON'T...

55

LOOK WHO'S HERE!
GUYS!
ELYON! IS YOUR DATE ALREADY OVER?

ONLY ROUND ONE! CEDRIC WANTS TO SEE ME TONIGHT IN THE *SCHOOL GYM*!
I CAN THINK OF MORE *ROMANTIC* PLACES!

HE SAID IT WAS THE PERFECT PLACE TO TELL ME A SPECIAL SECRET!

I GUESS THERE ARE LESS ***RIDICULOUS*** EXCUSES!

I DON'T SEE ANYONE! M-MAYBE IT'S ALL A BIG JOKE!
ELYON! ARE YOU HERE?
ELYON'S AT HOME SLEEPING, TRUST ME! IT'S PITCH-DARK IN HERE! LET'S GO!

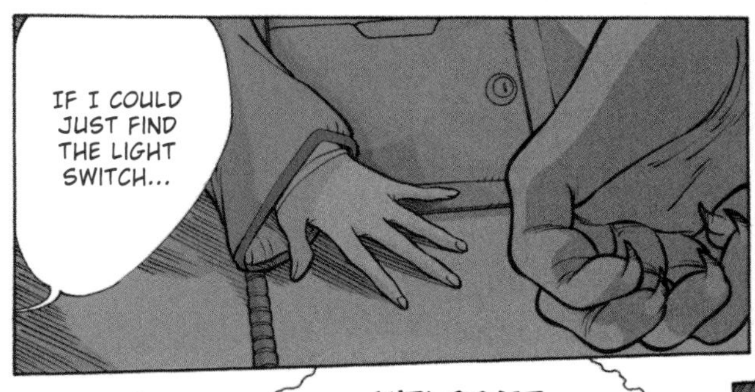
IF I COULD JUST FIND THE LIGHT SWITCH...

WELCOME, GUARDIANS!
PUT ME DOWN, YOU BIG APE! IF THIS IS A JOKE, IT'S NOT FUNNY!

AH!

WH-WHAT DO YOU WANT?
TO DESTROY YOU, GUARDIANS... TO DESTROY YOU AND TAKE OVER YOUR WORLD!
THE VEIL IS WEAK, AND WITHOUT YOU, VICTORY WILL BE FAR EASIER!
W-WEAK?
AT THE TURN OF EACH MILLENNIUM, ITS WEAVING LOOSENS...
...LIGHT FILTERS THROUGH ITS PORES, PIERCING OUR DARK-NESS...
IT IS THEN WE SEE THE PORTALS LEADING TO YOUR WORLD!
UGH!
WHAT SHALL I DO WITH THEM, SIR?
TEAR OPEN A PIT AND THROW THEM IN, VATHEK...
HEEELP!
THAT'S WHAT I FELT! THE HEART OF KANDRAKAR! MAYBE I SHOULD USE IT NOW?
HAY LIN! IRMA! WATER! AIR!
WH-WHAT'S HAPPENING TO US?

WE'VE GOT WINGS!
THIS IS MAGIC, HAY LIN!
BLASTED...! DESTROY THEM, VATHEK!
ZAP
TOO SLOW, BEAST!
KZ-ZASH

ZAM
WHOOOSH
HOLD ON, HAY LIN!
AAHH!
GET OUT OF THERE! FLY AWAY!
RIGHT! I CAN FLY! I'M AIR!
OUCH!
POWERS YOU DON'T KNOW HOW TO USE ARE WORTHLESS, LITTLE BIRD.
HEY!

KSSS
POWERS OF WATER, MIGHTY AND DEEP, WASH AWAY THIS STUPID CREEP!
WHOOSH

WHAT A LOUSY RHYME...
IT MAY BE MORE PATHETIC THAN POETIC, BUT I LIKE IT!
HURRY, GUYS! LET'S GET OUTTA HERE!

STOP! WHERE DO YOU THINK YOU'RE GOING?
WHO... WHO ARE YOU?

QUICKLY, SIR— *THE PORTAL CLOSES!*

IT IS NOT YET TIME, VATHEK!

NOW!

NOOO!

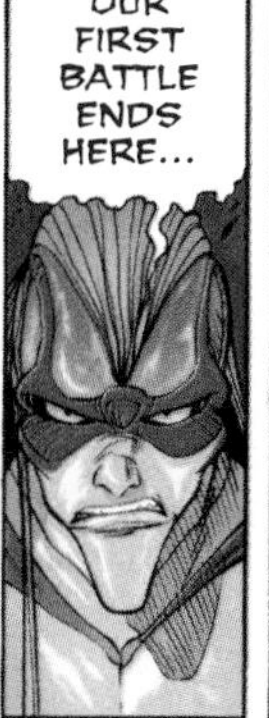

OUR FIRST BATTLE ENDS HERE...

...BUT THE COMING WAR WILL BE LONGER... AND MUCH MORE PAINFUL!

WE SHALL MEET AGAIN, WITCHES!

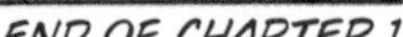
END OF CHAPTER 1

2

The Twelve Portals

HEATHERFIELD.
AS ITS NAME SUGGESTS, IT WAS ONCE FAMOUS FOR ITS FIELDS OF HEATHER...
WOOOOSH
WERE THERE SUCH A FIELD HERE, A BEAUTIFUL ARRAY OF COLORFUL FLOWERS WOULD BE ON DISPLAY, BUT INSTEAD, WE FIND ONLY WEEDS...

...AND SILENCE.

ANYBODY HOME?
LET'S FACE IT, GUYS...
...ELYON'S GONE!

BUT SHE COULDN'T HAVE VANISHED INTO THIN AIR...PEOPLE DON'T JUST DISAPPEAR LIKE THAT!
I SAY WE'LL SEE HER AGAIN.
HOW CAN YOU BE SO SURE?
I CAN FEEL IT, TARANEE! IT'S A SORT OF HUNCH...
...AFTER ALL, WE'RE ***WITCHES***, AREN'T WE?
RIGHT...

WHAT... WHAT ARE YOU DOING?
DON'T WORRY...

KWIN NNN

THIS WAY, IF SHE DECIDES TO COME BACK TOMORROW, SHE'LL HAVE A MORE ***COLORFUL*** WELCOME!

WHAT DO YOU THINK YOU'RE DOING? SOMEBODY COULD'VE SEEN YOU!
LUCKY NOBODY'S AROUND.

BUT THERE COULD'VE BEEN!
BUT THERE ISN'T!

BROMM

BRR-BROOOOOO
UH-OH... A STORM'S HEADING OUR WAY.
ANOTHER ONE...
...AND THIS TIME IT LOOKS NASTY! LET'S GO!

69

CORNELIA'S GOTTEN REALLY TOUCHY EVER SINCE SHE DISCOVERED HER POWERS...
I STILL CAN'T BELIEVE IT, HAY LIN...

...THIS IS REALLY HAPPENING TO US!

IT ALL STARTED A MONTH AGO...
...AND IN THE END, THE TWO MONSTERS VANISHED! IT WAS INCREDIBLE!
THE ONE WHO'S REALLY INCREDIBLE IS ELYON...
VENDO

SHE LED US STRAIGHT INTO A TRAP! THE "DATE" IN THE GYM WAS FOR US!
I TALKED TO CEDRIC, THAT GUY FROM THE BOOKSHOP...

...HE DIDN'T KNOW ANYTHING—HASN'T SEEN OR HEARD FROM HER SINCE THE PARTY...
SO SHE MADE IT ALL UP? BUT ***WHY***?

WE'LL ASK HER AS SOON AS SHE GETS BACK TO SCHOOL!
SHE HASN'T SHOWN UP FOR THREE DAYS, AND NOBODY ANSWERS AT HER HOUSE.

WHAT'S GOING ON, WILL?
DON'T ASK ME.

THE ANSWER'S ***HERE***!

YOUR GRANDMA'S STORY WAS TRUE. WE REALLY HAVE BECOME **MAGICAL**!
I DON'T BUY IT, HAY LIN!

BUT YOU'VE GOT TO BELIEVE, PLEASE! IF YOU JUST TRY...
TRY? TRY ***WHAT***, EXACTLY?

THAT, FOR EXAMPLE.

AH!

DID... DID I DO THAT?
YES, CORNELIA! THE ***POWERS OF EARTH*** ARE YOURS NOW...

...AND TARANEE, YOU HAVE THE POWER OF ***FIRE***!
HEY! BEFORE YOU DO ANYTHING, LET ME GET OUTTA THE WAY!
I'M REALLY ***SCARED***, WILL! I WANT TO ***UNDERSTAND*** ALL THIS!

UNDERSTANDING, YES...BUT THAT TAKES TIME...

HOW ABOUT A CUP OF TEA AT MY HOUSE?
OKAY!
NO THANKS. I CAN'T.

SEE YOU AT SCHOOL TOMORROW!
BYE!
LATER!
BUS

WHERE'S SHE RUNNING OFF TO?
HOME. HER GRANDMA'S PRETTY SICK, AND HAY LIN'S WORRIED ABOUT HER...

BRROOOOM

SHORTLY...
ANYBODY HOME?
NO. MY MOM'LL BE BACK IN A BIT. COME ON IN!

MAN, I'M BEAT!

UNDERSTANDABLE, GIVEN EVERYTHING THAT'S HAPPENED... BUT I WONDER IF WE'RE ALL TAKING THE WHOLE THING TOO LIGHTLY...

I MEAN, WE SHOULD BE TERRIFIED! WE'VE GOT MAGICAL POWERS! HAVE YOU NOTICED?

WE'RE CAUGHT UP IN SOMETHING INCREDIBLE BUT ACTING LIKE IT'S TOTALLY NORMAL!

WE FOUGHT A FRIEND WHO ***VANISHED INTO THIN AIR***, AND WE'RE HERE HAVING ***TEA***!

WHAT'S UP WITH THAT?

MAYBE WE'VE GOT A FEW ***SCREWS LOOSE*** BUT JUST NEVER REALIZED IT BEFORE...

SPEAK FOR YOURSELF, IRMA.

NO, THERE'S A LOT MORE TO THIS! I STILL DON'T GET **WHAT**, BUT THERE'S **SOMETHING**!
AS SOON AS HAY LIN'S GRANDMA GETS BETTER, WE'LL GO ASK HER A FEW QUESTIONS.

UNTIL THEN, WE BETTER WATCH OUR STEPS AND KEEP OUR EYES OPEN.

WIDE OPEN!
KRA-DOOOM

MINE ARE WIDE-OPEN, BUT I STILL CAN'T SEE ANYTHING!
THE LIGHTS WENT OUT, EINSTEIN!
DON'T MOVE! THERE SHOULD BE SOME CANDLES SOMEWHERE AROUND HERE!
DON'T BOTHER, WILL! I'LL TAKE CARE OF IT!
YEOW!
WOW! THEY DON'T BURN!
HA-HA! MY TURN, THEN! LEMME SHOW YOU GUYS SOMETHING!

ANYBODY WANT A SNACK?
HUH? LEARNED SOME NEW RECIPES?

WHAT CAN WE OFFER MY FRIENDS, JAMES?
JAMES? YOU'VE GOT A BUTLER AND NEVER TOLD US?

Not much, Miss Will, until someone restocks me.
AHHHH!

Allow me to point out that the cream cheese next to the pickles has long since expired.
THE FRIDGE CAN TALK!

SORRY, JAMES. I'LL GET RID OF IT RIGHT NOW.
DID YOU HEAR THAT? THE FRIDGE TALKS!
BIZARRE!

He has very refined senses, you know...
THE FRIDGE TALKS!
ALL RIGHT, ALREADY! I'M NOT DEAF!

I FOUND OUT YESTERDAY! I CAN TALK TO APPLIANCES! I NAMED EVERY ONE IN THE HOUSE!
AND THEY DO WHAT I TELL THEM! THEY EVEN WORK WITHOUT ELECTRICITY!
NOW THAT'S COST EFFICIENT! TURN ON CHANNEL 12! MARK COWET'S ON! HE'S THE HOTTEST VJ IN TV HISTORY!
HEAR THAT, BILLY?
No, no, no! Will, you know I can't bear the music he plays!
My poor speakers loathe that racket! What ever happened to the golden days of easy-listening music?
KSSKSKKSKSKSKSSK
BUT... BUT...
How about a nice documentary? There's one about the secret life of black bears on the Globe Channel!
Try to understand! He's a pretty old model!

YOU LEARN SOMETHING NEW EVERY DAY! GREAT, ISN'T IT?
...and in the winter months, the social life of larger plantigrade animals reaches decidedly low levels...
GRUNT

UM, SORRY TO ASK, WILL...I DON'T WANT TO IMPOSE, BUT...

...COULD I PRINT MY SCIENCE PAPER?
NO PROBLEM, TARANEE!

WAKE UP THE LITTLE WOMAN, GEORGE! THERE'S WORK TO BE DONE...
Work, work, work! That's all you want from me!

I need sleep too, y'know! Just 'cos I'm a machine doesn't mean you can treat me like this!
Aw, zip it, George! After all, I'm the one who's gotta do all the dirty work!
Don't talk to me like that, Mildred!
THEY'RE FIGHTING?
I THINK THEY'RE MARRIED. I COULD LISTEN TO THEM FOR HOURS.

ANOTHER CUP?

NO THANKS, WILL!
...and summertime is when the most reprobate of the black bears are at their worst...

SO WHAT DO YOU THINK KANDRAKAR IS? I MEAN, HOW DO YOU PICTURE THIS PLACE "IN THE MIDDLE OF INFINITY"?
YEAH...

...AND WHAT DANGERS ARE WE GOING TO HAVE TO FACE?

AND WHO WERE THOSE GUYS AT THE PARTY?

HOW ABOUT WE DO A LITTLE TRAINING OVER THE NEXT FEW DAYS? SURE, WE HAVE POWERS, BUT WE STILL DON'T KNOW HOW TO USE THEM.

CORNELIA'S RIGHT! IT'D BE TERRIBLE IF WE CREATED SOME KIND OF ***DISASTER*** JUST BECAUSE WE'RE ***INEXPERIENCED!***

ER...UM...SPEAKING OF WHICH, I WANTED TO TELL YOU GUYS SOMETHING...
OH, NO!

WHAT'S WRONG, WILL? WHAT DID YOU SEE?
ARE REPTILE GUY AND THE ***BLUE GORILLA*** BACK?

WORSE...

...MY MOM'S HOME!

THE SPHERES, TARANEE! ***PUT 'EM OUT, QUICK!***
FLAP FLAP
G-GOTCHA!

TELEVISION OFF!
FIZZ

SHUT DOWN, GEORGE!
One minute! One minute! Only six lines left... five lines...
BREE-BREEBREEE

...FOUR...
BREEEBREEE

KA BRAMM

...two... one...
REEEEEE
BREEEER
REEEP

TLAK

WILL, ARE YOU...?

UM... HI, MOM!
HIYA, MS. VANDOM! WANT SOME TEA?

MEANWHILE, AT HAY LIN'S...
BOOOM

ANYBODY HOME?

MOM? DAD? YOU THERE?

WHAT DO YOU THINK, DOCTOR?
?!

WHAT CAN I SAY, MR. LIN? LAST MONTH'S FLU TOOK ITS TOLL. SHE'S HAVING A HARD TIME RECOVERING...
MEDICINE WON'T HELP MUCH. THE TRUTH IS, YOUR MOTHER'S JUST VERY OLD. FRANKLY, SHE SEEMS TIRED.
I SEE...
WE'LL CONTINUE ALL THE TREATMENTS, BUT STAY BY HER SIDE. THAT'S WHAT SHE NEEDS MOST RIGHT NOW.

YOU KNOW WHAT I MEAN.
OF COURSE. THANK YOU SO MUCH...
DAD, I'M HOME!

HAY LIN, YOU'RE DRIPPING WET!
THIS ***YOUNG LADY*** CAN'T HAVE BEEN YOUR LITTLE GIRL.

GO CHANGE RIGHT NOW BEFORE YOU CATCH SOMETHING!
I'LL HURRY, PAPA...

A WARM BREEZE WOULD WORK BETTER THAN A HAIR DRYER, LITTLE ONE.
GRANDMA!

GO ON! NOW THAT YOUR FATHER ISN'T AROUND, LET ME SEE HOW YOU USE YOUR POWERS!
IF YOU SAY SO...

WHAT DO YOU THINK?
HA-HA! SPLENDID, MY BABY!

I THINK YOU'LL BECOME VERY GOOD!

THE WIND'S MY FRIEND, GRANDMA!
BUT FIRST YOU'LL HAVE TO PUT ON SOME WEIGHT IF YOU DON'T WANT A STORM CARRYING YOU OFF!

HOW DO YOU FEEL TODAY?
LET'S JUST SAY I'VE SEEN BETTER DAYS!

AND THE OTHER GUARDIANS OF THE VEIL ARE WELL?
FINE, GRANDMA... BUT YOU... YOU'LL GET BETTER, WON'T YOU?

OF COURSE! I FORESEE A GREAT IMPROVEMENT! HELP ME SIT UP, HAY LIN! THERE'S SOMETHING BENEATH MY PILLOW.
I SEE IT! IT'S...

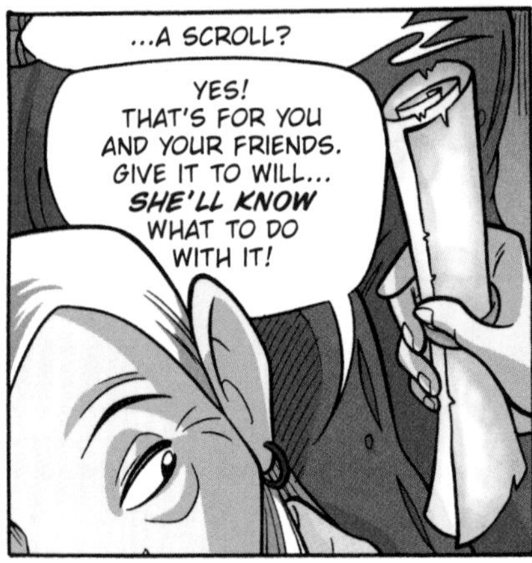
...A SCROLL?
YES! THAT'S FOR YOU AND YOUR FRIENDS. GIVE IT TO WILL... SHE'LL KNOW WHAT TO DO WITH IT!

WHAT'S WRITTEN ON IT?
IT'S A MAP OF THE TWELVE PORTALS, LITTLE ONE! THAT'S HOW MANY BREACHES THERE ARE IN THE VEIL...

...TWELVE PASSAGES THAT THE CREATURES OF METAMOOR WILL ATTEMPT TO USE TO ENTER OUR WORLD.
BUT... IT'S BLANK!

ARE YOU SURE, HAY LIN?
OH!
ZWIIIN

THIS IS HEATHERFIELD! AND THIS SHINY POINT...

Heatherfield

THAT'S YOUR **SCHOOL'S GYM**— WHERE THE FIRST BATTLE TOOK PLACE!

THAT WAS THE **FIRST PASSAGEWAY**! THE FLAMES SEALED IT, BUT YOU'LL HAVE TO DO THAT YOURSELVES FOR THE REST.

BUT THE MAP DOESN'T SHOW THEM... HOW CAN ANYONE USE A MAP LIKE THIS?

AS I'VE ALREADY TOLD YOU AND YOUR FRIENDS— YOU'LL LEARN EVERYTHING WITH TIME.

I WAS ALSO ONCE A GUARDIAN OF THE **VEIL**, LONG BEFORE YOU. AND I WAS ONCE JUST AS IMPATIENT AS YOU ARE NOW.

YOU WERE A WITCH TOO?

A WITCH? **HA-HA-HA!** I KNOW THAT'S WHAT YOU CALL THEM THESE DAYS...

...BUT WE AREN'T **WITCHES**, DEAR. WE'RE SOMETHING **DIFFERENT**!

THOUGH IN MY CASE, I'M NOT REALLY ANYTHING ANYMORE. IT'S YOUR TURN NOW, HAY LIN.
TIME FOR YOUR MEDICINE, MOM!

AND NO COMPLAINTS! I TRIED IT MYSELF, AND IT'S VERY TASTY!
IF IT'S SO GOOD, WHY DON'T YOU ADD IT TO TODAY'S ***MENU***?

ENOUGH OF THAT. DON'T MAKE A SCENE IN FRONT OF YOUR GRANDDAUGHTER.
ONCE I WAS THE ONE TAKING CARE OF YOU, YOUNG MAN...

...BUT IT NEVER CROSSED MY MIND TO FORCE YOU TO SWALLOW SOMETHING SO NASTY!
COME ON, NOW...

SEE? IT WASN'T SO BAD AFTER ALL.
BLEAH

TAKE CARE, HAY LIN— AND PROMISE ME YOU'LL ***EAT***!
I PROMISE!

GOOD NIGHT, GRANDMA.

KANDRAKAR

SO OUR GUARDIANS HAVE THE MAP OF THE TWELVE PORTALS.
HONORABLE *YAN LIN* HAS DONE TRULY EXCELLENT WORK, ORACLE.

YES—AND THAT MEANS HER MISSION HAS ENDED.
UNDER-STOOD, SIR.

87

YOU KNOW WHAT TO DO, TIBOR. INFORM THE COUNCIL.

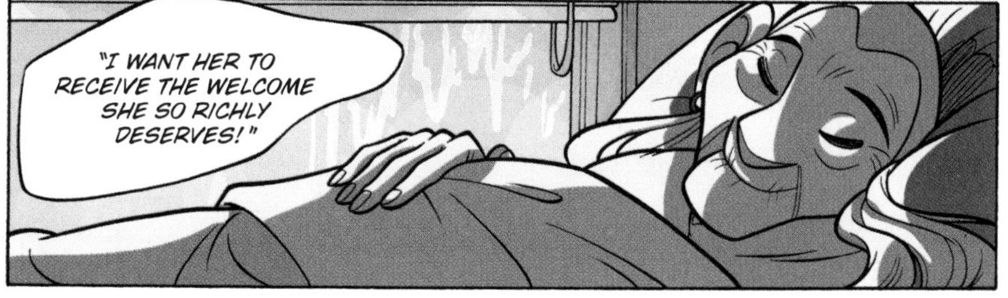
"I WANT HER TO RECEIVE THE WELCOME SHE SO RICHLY DESERVES!"

THE NEXT MORNING AT SHEFFIELD INSTITUTE
DID YOU HEAR THE NEWS? EVERYONE'S TALKING!
HUH?
THE POLICE ARE IN THE PRINCIPAL'S OFFICE! I SAW TWO COPS A FEW MINUTES AGO!
POOR MS. KNICKERBOCHER! SHE'S MEAN, BUT NOT MEAN ENOUGH TO GET SENT TO JAIL!
SORRY TO DISAPPOINT YOU, HAY LIN! DIDN'T YOU WATCH THE NEWS THIS MORNING?
NO... WHY? WHAT HAPPENED?
IT'S IN THE PAPERS AND EVERYTHING! A BOY FROM OUR SCHOOL DISAPPEARED!
YEAH! ANDREW HORNBY! EVER MET HIM?
WHO? THAT GORGEOUS BLOND GUY FROM CLASS 5D?!
EXACTLY! HE HASN'T BEEN HOME FOR THREE DAYS, SO AS OF LAST NIGHT, HE'S OFFICIALLY A MISSING PERSON!

IRMA! ISN'T THAT THE GUY YOU'RE CRAZY ABOUT?
ANDREW
WELL, Y-YOU COULD SAY THAT...

LISTEN, I'VE BEEN TRYING TO TELL YOU GUYS SOMETHING SINCE LAST NIGHT...
LOOK! THEY'RE COMING OUT!

I'D APPRECIATE THAT, OFFICER. GOOD LUCK!
THANKS FOR EVERYTHING, MA'AM. WE'LL KEEP YOU POSTED.
ckerbocker
RINCIPAL
POLIC

SEE? THEY DIDN'T ARREST HER.
NOT YET.

89

HAY LIN, I NEED A WORD WITH YOU.
DID SHE HEAR ME?

WOULD YOU COME INTO MY OFFICE FOR A MOMENT, PLEASE?

I CAN EXPLAIN EVERYTHING, MS. KNICKERBOCHER! IT WAS JUST A LITTLE JOKE, AND...
SIT DOWN, HAY LIN. I...I DON'T KNOW HOW TO TELL YOU THIS...

BEFORE THE POLICE ARRIVED, YOUR FATHER CALLED. HE'S COMING TO PICK YOU UP.

DID...DID SOMETHING HAPPEN...?

Mrs. Knickerbocker
PRINCIPAL

THE SCENT RISING FROM THE INCENSE IS UNUSUALLY DELICATE AS IT DRIFTS ON THE WIND...

...THE SAME WIND THAT BILLOWS ACROSS HEATHERFIELD CEMETERY.

AT CHINESE FUNERALS, WHITE IS THE COLOR OF MOURNING. THE FLOWERS AND PAPER RIBBONS GIVE THE ILLUSION OF SNOW.

THOUGH IT ISN'T SNOWING, A CHILL LINGERS.

91

GO AHEAD.

THANKS FOR COMING, GUYS.
HAY LIN...

I LOVE YOU ALL!

?

IT CAN'T BE!

93

ELYON!

I SAW ELYON! SHE'S DOWN THERE!
!

WHAT ARE YOU TALKING ABOUT? **WHERE?**
SHE WAS THERE! I SAW HER!

ELYON!

IT WAS ***HER***, I SWEAR! SHE COULDN'T HAVE HIDDEN THAT QUICK!
LET'S GO TAKE A LOOK. MAYBE IT WAS JUST...

UHNNN!
WILL! ARE YOU OKAY?

NO, I DON'T THINK SO...

NEVER MIND. I'M OKAY NOW! IT'S ALL GOOD.
HAY LIN, FUNERALS MESS WITH PEOPLE. YOU PROBABLY JUST MADE A MISTAKE. IT'S UNDERSTANDABLE... LET'S GET OUT OF HERE.
EXCELLENT, ELYON!
EXCELLENT!

IT'S A NEW DAY IN HEATHERFIELD...

LAIR

ANY WORD ABOUT THIS BOY AT THE STATION?
NOT YET, BUT THERE'S OTHER NEWS! SERGEANT SOMMER JUST CALLED...

THE POLICE IN AUBRY FOUND YOUR FRIEND ELYON'S PARENTS' CAR.
REALLY?

YUP. BUT THERE'S STILL NO TRACE OF THE GIRL OR HER FAMILY. VANISHED INTO THIN AIR...
AUBRY'S PRETTY FAR FROM HERE. WHAT WERE THEY DOING OVER THERE?

WE'LL FIND OUT SOON ENOUGH. SEE YOU LATER, LADIES!
HAVE A GOOD DAY, TOM!

HMMM... THE PLOT THICKENS...
MISSING
Have you seen this boy?
Andrew Hornby
CEREAL

"I'VE GOTTA TALK TO THE GUYS RIGHT AWAY!"

MAYBE MOM WAS RIGHT... THIS PLACE ISN'T SO BAD AFTER ALL!

IF THE STUPID CRITTER'D JUST LET ME GRAB HIM! COME HERE...
AH-HA! GOT 'IM!

YAAAGH!
HEH-HEH-HEH! NOW *THIS* IS WHAT I CALL FUN!

AHHH! GET IT OFF ME! LEGGO MY FINGER, YOU LITTLE RAT!
BOUMP

THUNK
LET GO!

99

YOU ROTTEN LITTLE...
?
?
DON'T YOU DARE!

OH-HO, THE **NEW GIRL'S** GOT GUTS!
WHAT'S YOUR PROBLEM?

IDIOTS! PICKING ON GIRLS AND DEFENSELESS ANIMALS! SHOULDA SOCKED HIM!
?
?

IF THEY TRY THAT AGAIN, I SWEAR I'LL **ZAP** 'EM!

YOU ALL RIGHT, LITTLE FELLA?
RRRR!

CHOMP
OW!

HEY! UNGRATEFUL PIPSQUEAK! I RESCUE YOU, AND THIS IS THE THANKS I GET?
?
?
?

NEED A HAND?
YOU AGAIN...
?

I CAN MANAGE, THANKS!
OUCH!
POW

WH-WHAT'S YOUR PROBLEM?
OHMIGOSH! SORRYSORRY SORRY! M-MY BAD!

I'M SORRY! I DIDN'T MEAN TO! I...I THOUGHT YOU WERE SOMEONE ELSE!
DORMICE HAVE A MEAN SIDE TO THEM, BUT YOU'RE PRETTY TOUGH YOURSELF!

YOU'RE MATT, RIGHT? I REALLY LIKED YOU AT THE HALLOWEEN CONCERT! THAT IS...I MEAN... I LIKED YOUR SINGING!
THANKS!

MY NAME'S WILL.
AND THIS IS YOUR LITTLE PET, HUH? LOOKS LIKE HE CAME OUT OF HIBERNATION A BIT TOO EARLY...
BUMP

LOOK HOW OUT OF IT HE IS! DAZED, COLD, HUNGRY...
OW! AW!
?

THIS'LL MAKE HIM FEEL BETTER.
WHAT HE NEEDS IS A NICE, COZY NEST! AN OLD SOCK AND A T-SHIRT SHOULD DO THE TRICK!
?
HE'LL SNUGGLE UP INSIDE AND POP OUT ONCE IN A WHILE WHEN HE FEELS LIKE EATING SOMETHING.
?
SOUNDS LIKE YOU KNOW ALL ABOUT THIS STUFF!
MY GRANDPA HAS A PET SHOP, BUT DON'T ASK ME TO TAKE HIM THERE. THE OLD GUY'S BUSY ENOUGH WITH ALL THE ANIMALS HE ALREADY HAS!
HOLD ON! I CAN'T KEEP HIM!
ARE YOU KIDDING? YOU TWO WERE CLEARLY MADE FOR EACH OTHER!
SEE YOU AT SCHOOL! AND IF YOU NEED ANY DORMOUSE ADVICE...
...HERE'S MY NUMBER.

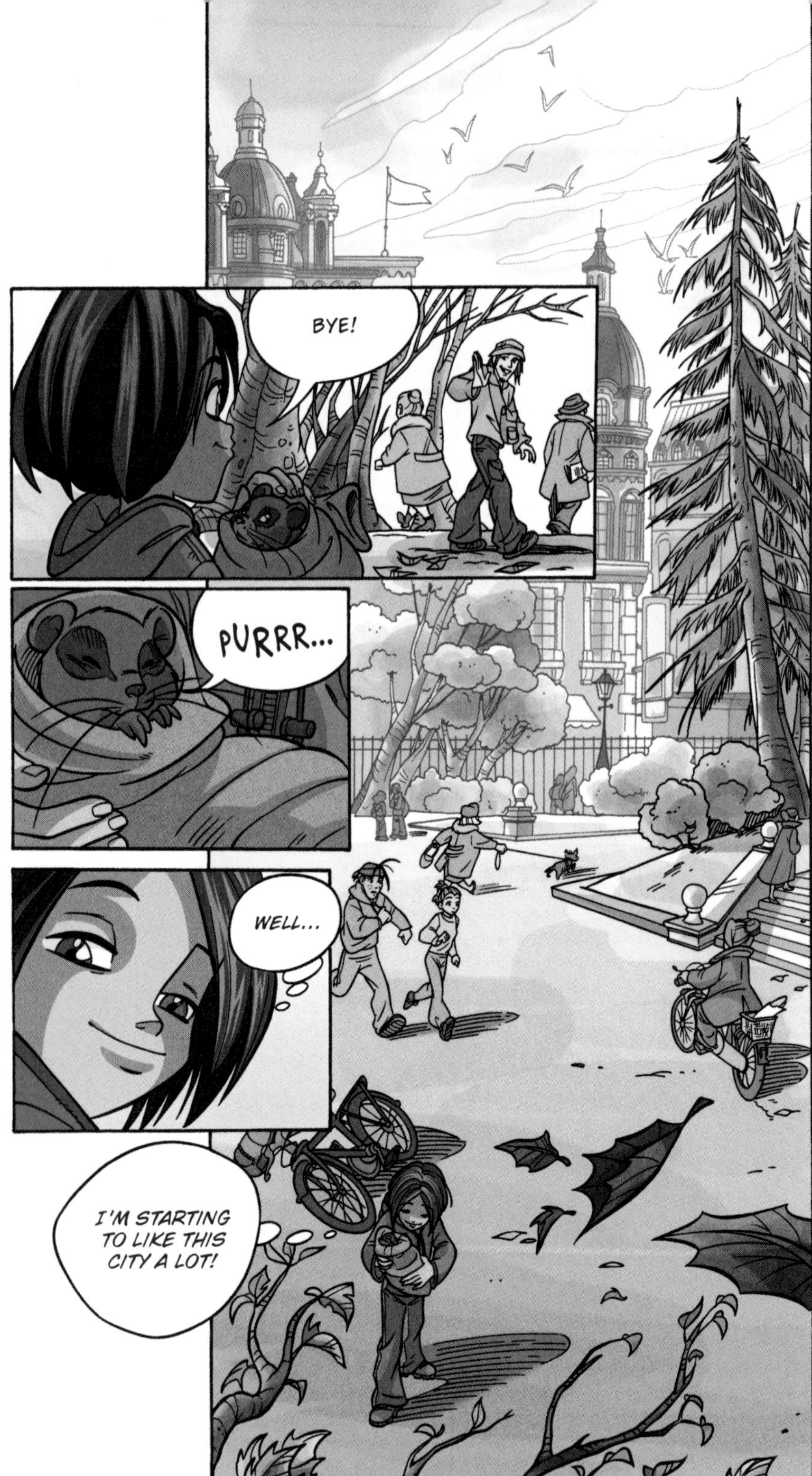
BYE!
PURRR...
WELL...
I'M STARTING TO LIKE THIS CITY A LOT!

LATER...
...AND THAT'S ALL I FOUND OUT.
AUBRY, HUH? THAT'S NEAR THE BORDER. THINK THEY'RE RUNNING AWAY FROM SOMETHING?

PUMPKIN CAFETERIA
COULD BE— BUT WHAT?
WHO KNOWS? WE WERE IN THE SAME CLASS TOGETHER FOR THREE YEARS, BUT ELYON NEVER TOLD ME MUCH ABOUT HER FAMILY.

MAYBE THERE'S A CONNECTION BETWEEN ELYON'S DISAPPEARANCE AND THAT BOY'S. WHAT DO YOU GUYS THINK?
THAT'S A POSSIBILITY!

105

I DON'T THINK SO!
HOW CAN YOU BE SO SURE?
LIST

'COS...WELL...I'VE BEEN TRYING TO TELL YOU GUYS FOR A FEW DAYS NOW... AND...SEE...I DON'T KNOW HOW TO EXPLAIN IT, BUT...

...I KNOW WHAT HAPPENED TO ANDREW HORNBY!
WHAAAT? WHY DIDN'T YOU TELL US BEFORE?

BECAUSE I'M THE ONE WHO MADE HIM DISAPPEAR!
MAN, IRMA! WHAT KIND OF MESS DID YOU GET YOURSELF INTO THIS TIME?
I REALLY LIKED HIM... ANDREW... Y'KNOW, BUT HE NEVER EVEN LOOKED AT ME, SO...
SO...?
IT HAPPENED ABOUT A WEEK AGO! DO YOU KNOW THE ZOT, THAT CLUB NEAR THE SQUARE? WELL, THERE WAS THIS PARTY...
I KNEW ANDREW WAS GOING! IT WAS MY CHANCE TO GET HIM TO NOTICE ME, SO...
DON'T SAY IT... DON'T SAY IT... DON'T SAY IT...
...I TRANSFORMED!
SHE SAID IT!
"MY PARENTS HAD BEEN ASLEEP FOR A WHILE—ALL I HAD TO DO WAS THINK IT...
"AND VOILÀ! MAKEOVER!

106

"I HID MY WINGS AND SNEAKED INTO THE PARTY! YOU SHOULD'VE SEEN IT! I TURNED EVERY HEAD!"
PARTY
THE ZOT
ZOT
ZOT

INCLUDING ANDREW'S?
ESPECIALLY HIS! WE TALKED AND DANCED ALL NIGHT! IT WAS FANTASTIC!

I CAN'T BELIEVE IT! YOU USED YOUR POWERS FOR A PARTY?!
I DIDN'T THINK I WAS DOING ANYTHING WRONG!

AND THEN? GET TO THE POINT, IRMA!
WELL, WHEN WE LEFT, ANDREW OFFERED ME A RIDE HOME IN HIS CAR, AND I ACCEPTED!

BUT ALL OF A SUDDEN, HE PULLED THE CAR OVER AND... AND...TRIED TO KISS ME!

AND ......?
YOU SURE YOU WANNA KNOW?

"I TURNED HIM INTO A TOAD!"
FZZZ
ZAP

ANYTHING WRONG, HOT STUFF?
MARTIN, DISAPPEA—

!
IRMA, NO! DON'T SAY IT!

UM, WOULD YOU KINDLY SHOVE OFF, MARTY?
YOUR WISH IS MY COMMAND, SUGAR PLUM!

SO WHAT DO WE DO NOW?
SIMPLE! WE HAVE TO FIND ANDREW RIGHT AWAY AND...

109

UHNN...
WILL! ARE YOU HAVING THAT FUNNY FEELING AGAIN? SHOULD WE START WORRYING?

IT'S LIKE A SHIVER—A DIZZY SPELL—LIKE I'M FALLING INTO NOTHING-NESS!

NO!

WHAT IS IT, HAY LIN?

I'LL OPEN THE EMERGENCY EXIT!

THIS WAY! IT LOOKS LIKE THE BACK DOOR'S OPEN!
ARE WE SURE WE SHOULD BE DOING THIS? THIS IS UNLAWFUL ENTRY!

MY MOTHER'S A JUDGE, AND MY FATHER USED TO BE A LAWYER! I'M TELLING YOU, THIS COULD GET US IN SERIOUS TROUBLE!
IF YOU AREN'T UP FOR IT, NOBODY'S FORCING YOU! JUST WAIT HERE!

HEH HEH HEH!
YOU WANT ME TO STAY HERE ALL ALONE? FORGET IT!

WOW!

112

IT LOOKS SO MUCH SMALLER FROM THE OUTSIDE!
WHICH WAY DO WE GO?

THAT WAY!
FRUP

FRUP
FRUP
FRUP
HEY, LOOK AT THOSE...
...FOOT-PRINTS!

THEY'RE HEADING TOWARD THE BASEMENT!
LOOKS LIKE AN INVITATION TO ME!

GIVE US SOME LIGHT, TARANEE.

WITH PLEASURE!

YOU STAY HERE AND DON'T GO ANYWHERE, LITTLE FELLA. I'LL BE RIGHT BACK!

RRRR-RRON! ZZZ!

THERE'S NO SIGN OF THE FOOTPRINTS!
AND THIS BASEMENT DOESN'T HAVE ANY **DOORS**! WHERE WERE THEY TRYING TO LEAD US?

TO ME, GIRLS...

...COME GET ME!
ELYON! CAN...CAN YOU HEAR US?

COME GET ME... COME GET ME...

DONG
ANOTHER WALL! THIS IS BECOMING A HABIT!

DONG DONG DONG
WHAT THE...?

IT'S METAL!
LET ME TAKE A LOOK!

THERE'S A DOOR UNDERNEATH!
SCRATCH SCRATCH

OH, RIGHT! IT'S MY GRANDMOTHER'S CHART—***THE MAP OF THE TWELVE PORTALS!***
WHERE'D THAT COME FROM? WHY DIDN'T YOU TELL US ABOUT IT?
I WOULD HAVE, BUT I WAS UPSET, WITH THE FUNERAL AND EVERYTHING, AND IT TOTALLY SLIPPED MY MIND!
IT'S A MAP OF THE CITY! AND THESE SHINY POINTS...

THEY'RE THE PASSAGEWAYS LEADING TO ***METAMOOR***! THE BREACHES THAT, AS ***GUARDIANS OF THE VEIL***, WE HAVE TO CLOSE! THE FIRST WAS THE ONE IN THE GYM.
School
Elyon
AND THIS OTHER ONE?

IT'S ELYON'S HOUSE! ***AND HERE WE ARE, GUYS!***

VRAAAAM
AH!

IT'S A TRAP!
DO SOMETHING, CORNELIA!

AHHH! GET ME OUT OF HERE!
THUMP THUMP

WHAT ARE YOU AFRAID OF HAY LIN?

I'M YOUR FRIEND. FOLLOW ME! COME WITH ME TO THE OTHER SIDE!
NO... YOU'RE NOT REAL...THIS IS JUST A NIGHT-MARE!

NO, NO, YOUNG LADY! IT'S ALL REAL!
?

AND THIS TIME, YOU WON'T ESCAPE! YOUR LITTLE ADVENTURE IS AT AN END!
EEEEK!

EEEEK!
OH NO! HAY LIN'S IN TROUBLE!
STAND BACK! I'LL KNOCK THE WALL DOWN!

IT'S POINTLESS TO FIGHT!
AHHH!
KRRRR
UNNNNGH!
IT'S POINTLESS TO RESIST!
... POINTLESS...
N-NO! NOOOO!
IT CAN'T END LIKE THIS! THE HEART OF KANDRAKAR...
...OUR POWERS... AT THEIR VERY STRONGEST!

"WATER...
"FIRE...
YESSS!
"EARTH...
"...AND AIR!"

FREE...

...STRONG...

...AND ANGRY!

121

ALL GOOD, GUYS?

IT'S INCREDIBLE! I'M...I'M DIFFERENT!

COOL, RIGHT? TOLD YA! AND NOW COMES THE BEST PART!

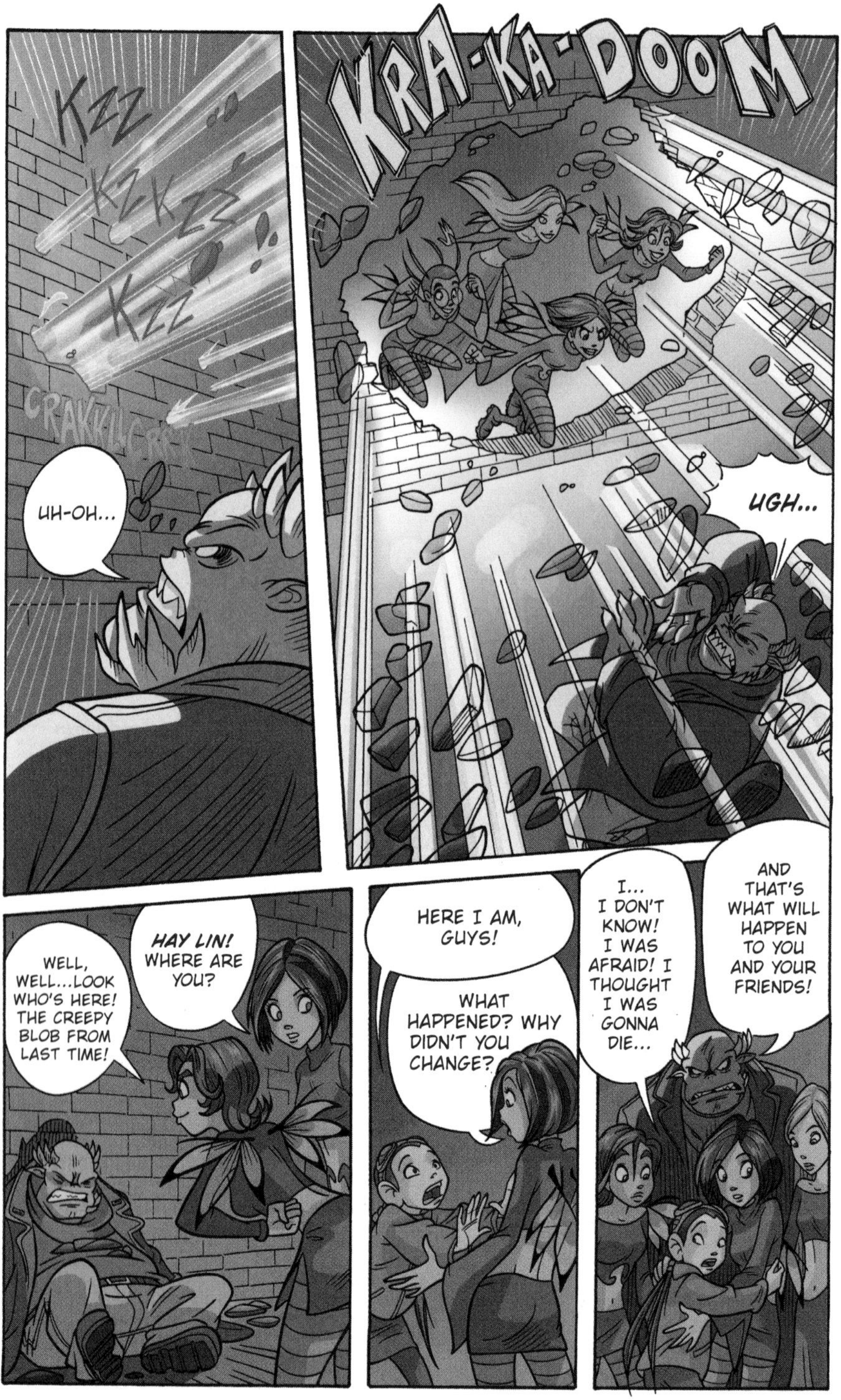

KZZ
KZKZZ
KZZ
CRAKKLCRET
UH-OH...
KRA-KA-DOOM
UGH...
HAY LIN! WHERE ARE YOU?
WELL, WELL...LOOK WHO'S HERE! THE CREEPY BLOB FROM LAST TIME!
HERE I AM, GUYS!
WHAT HAPPENED? WHY DIDN'T YOU CHANGE?
I... I DON'T KNOW! I WAS AFRAID! I THOUGHT I WAS GONNA DIE...
AND THAT'S WHAT WILL HAPPEN TO YOU AND YOUR FRIENDS!

NO—
TO YOU!
WAMM

HEY! NOT TOO SHABBY FOR AN AMATEUR!
ENOUGH! **ENOUGH! STOP IT!**

WHY ARE YOU DOING THIS?
IS THAT YOU, ELYON? TALK TO US, PLEASE...

YOU'RE FIGHTING A USELESS BATTLE, AND BY THE TIME YOU FINALLY UNDERSTAND THAT, IT'LL BE **TOO LATE**!
WAIT! WHAT DO YOU MEAN?

TOO LATE.

KWAAM

WHAT DID SHE MEAN BY THAT?
I DON'T KNOW, TARANEE. I FEEL MORE CLUELESS BY THE DAY...
WHERE'D ELYON GO? AND WHAT DOES ANY OF THIS MEAN?
MAYBE THAT BIG BOOK'LL HELP US! IT WAS HIDDEN DOWN THERE!
THERE'S NOTHING ELSE?
NOPE— TOTALLY EMPTY!
ALL THINGS CONSIDERED, WE DIDN'T DO SO BAD FOR COMPLETE BEGINNERS!
YEAH, BUT WE'RE STILL UNPREPARED. WE SURVIVED AGAIN, BUT WE DON'T KNOW **HOW**!
IF WE WANT TO FULFILL OUR MISSION, WE'VE GOT TO **STUDY**...
AS IF HOMEWORK **WASN'T BAD ENOUGH!**
FROM NOW ON, WE CAN'T MAKE ANY MORE MISTAKES!
RIGHT... WH-WHY ARE YOU LOOKIN' AT ME?

EPILOGUE
THE MARSHES OF HEATHERFIELD

MAN! ALL THESE MOSQUITOES! SHOULDN'T THEY BE ON VACATION THIS TIME OF YEAR?
BZZZzz BZZZ

THE PROBLEM'S THAT THE SEASONS ARE CHANGING! MY DAD THINKS SO TOO, AND HE SAYS IT'S ALL BECAUSE...

SPAT
!

HEY!
YOU HAD ONE ON YOUR NECK!

COME ON, GUYS, LET'S NOT WASTE ANY MORE TIME!
A TOAD? REALLY? COULDN'T YOU HAVE CHANGED THE GUY INTO SOMETHING MORE OBVIOUS? LOOK AT US—UP TO OUR EARS IN SWAMP WATER, THANKS TO YOUR LITTLE PRANK!

END OF CHAPTER 2

13

THE DARK DIMENSION

bi-bip bi-bip bi-bip bi-bip bi-bip

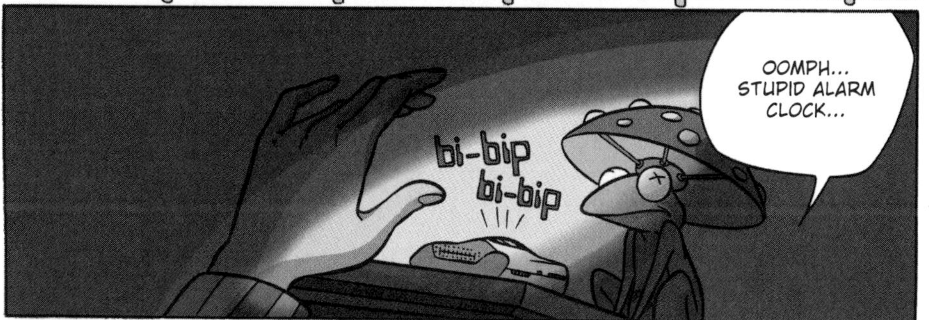

bi-bip
bi-bip
OOMPH... STUPID ALARM CLOCK...

I'M NOT EVEN UP YET AND ALREADY FEEL TIRED!

GUESS MOM'S RIGHT...I SHOULD GO TO BED EARLIER. I KNOW EXACTLY WHAT SHE'LL SAY...
"WILL, LOOK AT YOUR FACE IN THE MIRROR...
"...YOU LOOK SO PALE THIS MORNING..."
!

WH-WHAT HAPPENED TO ME?
WHERE'S MY FACE?
WILL! BREAKFAST'S READY!
I-I'M COMING, MOM!
CAN'T GO OUT LIKE THIS!
GOTTA DO SOME-THING!
MY MARKERS! IT'D BE EASY...
...IF MY HAND WOULD STOP SHAKING! AND THE NOSE IS TOO BIG!
I HATE IT! I HATE IT!
CLUNK

IT'S NOT ME! NOT ME AT ALL!

N-NOBODY...

NOBODY'LL RECOGNIZE ME...

OMPH!

KBUMP

YOU! THERE! GET OVER HERE, NOW!

I HAD A HORRIBLE NIGHT, AND IT'S YOUR FAULT!

YOU'VE BEEN RUNNING AROUND ALL NIGHT LONG!

LOOK AT THIS MESS! I JUST CLEANED THIS PLACE TWO DAYS AGO!

IF YOU'RE GONNA LIVE HERE, YOU GOTTA KNOW ONE RULE: KEEP. YOUR. PAWS. OFF. MY. STUFF. OKAY?
KIRRRR!
KLUMP
MAN... YOU'RE HOPELESS!
THUMP
Clean this mess later, Will! You've got an appointment, remember? And you're late — as usual!
SHOOT, YOU'RE RIGHT! THANKS, CLOCK...
WILL! BREAKFAST'S READY!
UH... COMING, MOM!
WHO WERE YOU TALKING TO?
TALKING TO...? AH...UH... TO HIM!
I WAS SCOLDING HIM! LOOK WHAT HE DID!
UH... ARE YOU SURE IT WAS ALL HIS FAULT?
DORMICE ARE PRETTY FAMOUS FOR SLEEPING A LOT.
WELL, NOT HIM!

AND MESSY DAUGHTERS SHOULDN'T TELL LIES!
BUT IT'S TRUE! ***TELL HER IT'S TRUE!***

BREAKFAST'S READY!
GRUNT
WE'LL SETTLE THIS WHEN I GET BACK!

GOING OUT?
YUP! GOTTA MEET MY FRIENDS!

I WAS HOPING WE COULD TALK, WILL. IT'S SUNDAY— THE ONE DAY WE GET TO SPEND TIME TOGETHER!

WE'LL TALK TONIGHT, OKAY?
I...OKAY.

A SUNDAY LIKE ANY OTHER, EXCEPT...
NOW WATCH...
WOOOOSH
KRRRR
WELL? WHADDAYA THINK?
WOW!
NOT BAD...
THUMP
NOT BAD?
I CAN DO SOMETHING BETTER...
OH, OF COURSE! MISS KNOW-IT-ALL ALWAYS CAN!
OF COURSE I CAN, IRMA...
MISS KNOW-IT-ALL CAN ALWAYS DO BETTER! EVERYBODY HEAR THAT...?
SHUT UP AND WATCH...
KSHH
...BET YOU CAN'T DO THAT!
OH! AMAZING! NEVER SEEN ANYTHING SO LAME IN MY LIFE...
THUMP

OH, COME ON... WOULD YOU TWO QUIT BICKERING? WE'RE HERE TO PRACTICE!
WILL'S RIGHT! WE SHOULD HELP EACH OTHER! WE'RE A **TEAM**, NOW...
SURE...BUT WE DON'T KNOW HOW OUR POWERS WORK YET. IF ONLY GRANDMA'D TOLD US MORE...
WE'LL HAVE TO MAKE DO WITHOUT HER. THAT'S ALL.
YOU REALLY THINK THAT'S GOOD ENOUGH? I MEAN... LOOK AROUND, BOSS!
WE CAN DO MAGIC! WE CAN TRANSFIGURE THINGS! WE COMMAND WATER, AIR, EARTH AND FIRE...BUT WE DON'T KNOW **WHY**!
WELL... WE'RE THE GUARDIANS OF THE VEIL!
I KNOW THAT! **BUT WHY?** WHY US...?
'COS WE'RE SOOO PRETTY! DON'CHA THINK?
I'M NOT JOKING, IRMA!

OUR LIVES HAVE CHANGED, WILL... BUT WE DIDN'T CHOOSE THIS!
YOU'RE RIGHT, CORNELIA. I DON'T KNOW WHAT TO SAY. I'M AS LOST AS YOU.

I THOUGHT OUR **LEADER** HAD ALL THE ANSWERS!
WELL, I DON'T! IN FACT, I'M NOT EVEN SURE I'M YOUR LEADER! LIKE YOU SAID... ***WE DIDN'T CHOOSE THIS!***

I'M SURE THIS **BOOK** HAS THE SOLUTION TO ALL OUR PROBLEMS...
WRONG, HAY LIN! THAT BOOK'S JUST ***ONE MORE*** PROBLEM!

DID YOU MANAGE TO OPEN IT?
NO WAY— AND I TRIED EVERYTHING! ***IT'S NAILED SHUT!***
THERE'S... THERE'S ***A SPELL*** ON THAT BOOK...

PUT IT AWAY!
ARE YOU HAVING THAT STRANGE FEELING AGAIN?

UH...IT'S SO BIZARRE! I FEEL DIZZY...GET BUTTERFLIES IN MY STOMACH...WELL, I GUESS I'LL GET USED TO IT EVENTUALLY!
MAYBE IT'S SOMETHING YOU HAD FOR BREAKFAST.
HA-HA-HA! I DON'T THINK SO! IT DOESN'T LAST LONG...AND IT'S HARD TO DESCRIBE!
IT'S LIKE...THE FEELING I GET WHENEVER I GET CALLED TO THE BLACK-BOARD IN MATH!
AH! THAT MEANS YOU'RE SCARED!
WAIT A MINUTE! MAYBE OUR MATH TEACHER'S A CREATURE FROM METAMOOR?
WHO? MS. RUDOLPH? SHE'S SO NICE!
THINGS AREN'T ALWAYS WHAT THEY SEEM, TARANEE! DEVOTING YOUR WHOLE LIFE TO MATH IS JUST INHUMAN!
HA-HA-HA!

ANYWAY, GUYS—BREAK'S OVER! LET'S GO AGAIN.
SURE! I WANNA TEST OUT A **COMBO**! COME ON, LET'S TRY!
I WONDER WHAT HAPPENS IF WE COMBINE...LET'S SEE... THE POWERS OF **WATER** AND **EARTH**!
THAT'S THE POWER OF **MUD**!
I'LL GO FIRST!
NO! ME!
BZ-ZAP
KZ-ZAP
FWOOOM
UH-OH...
BROUMBLE

SEE WHAT YOU DID?

POOR GIRL! YOU'RE GONNA NEED A BARREL OF CONDITIONER!

STOP!

KWIIIN

FWOOSH

YIKES!

AH!

OOMPH...

-PANT-

BLUBB
BLUB
GLUB

...WHAT WERE WE TALKING ABOUT?

3A
WHAT MAKES MONDAY THE WORST DAY OF THE WHOLE WEEK? MS. RUDOLPH'S TWO-HOUR MATH CLASS. THOSE LAST TWO HOURS JUST DRAG BY...
WOULD YOU CARE TO JOIN US, WILL?
UH?
Will! She's talking to you!
AS IF MATH WASN'T BAD ENOUGH!
SORRY, I DIDN'T HEAR YOU, MA'AM! I WASN'T LISTENING!
THAT'S WHY I CALLED ON YOU. YOU MUST KNOW YOUR LESSON QUITE WELL, SINCE YOU CAN AFFORD NOT TO PAY ATTENTION!
WE WERE REVIEWING RUFFINI'S THEOREM! WOULD YOU LIKE TO TAKE OVER?
UH...WELL... GLADLY! WELL... THE THEOREM OF...WHAT'S THE NAME?
RUFFINI, WILL! BINOMIALS... POLYNOMIALS... X SQUARED...
OH, SURE... GOT IT!

WELL...RUFFINI'S THEOREM, LET ME SEE...HMM...
TAKE YOUR TIME. WE'RE IN NO HURRY. WE HAVE A GOOD **FIFTEEN MINUTES** BEFORE THE END OF THE LESSON...

FIFTEEN MINUTES CAN BE A LONG, LONG TIME, MY FRIEND, BUT... AS THEY SAY...

DRIIING
...TIME FLIES WHEN YOU'RE HAVING **FUN**!

BYE, MA'AM!
BUT...HEY! WAIT **A MINUTE**! WHERE ARE YOU GOING?
SEE YOU, MS. RUDOLPH!
?
BRRRRRRUMBLE

EXTRAORDINARY! THE BELL RANG EARLY TODAY!
SAVED BY THE BELL, HUH?
Thanks!
You owe me one!

WELL... ALL RIGHT, THEN... BYE, MS. RUDOLPH!
WAIT A MINUTE, WILL!
YOU HADN'T LEARNED YOUR LESSON, HAD YOU?
IT'S...IT'S JUST THAT THEOREM! I TRIED... NOT MUCH, THAT'S TRUE... BUT I TRIED! I REALLY JUST DON'T GET IT!
HOW ARE YOU GETTING ON IN HEATHERFIELD, WILL? I MEAN...IS EVERYTHING ALL RIGHT?
YOU'VE BEEN HERE A MONTH NOW.
SURE! WHY DO YOU ASK?
I KNOW MATH ISN'T MUCH FUN, BUT I NOTICED THAT YOU ALWAYS LOOK SO PENSIVE AND DISTANT...
THINGS AREN'T SO EASY FOR ME RIGHT NOW... BUT I'M FINE.
I'M GLAD. BY THE WAY... I COULD HELP YOU WITH THAT THEOREM, IF YOU LIKE.
I DON'T USUALLY GIVE PRIVATE LESSONS, BUT I COULD MAKE AN EXCEPTION FOR YOU IF IT HELPS YOU BE MORE ATTENTIVE DURING MY LESSONS...
I... THANK YOU SO MUCH, MA'AM!

Sheffield Institute
ANY AFTERNOON WILL DO. WHAT DO YOU THINK? I'M SURE AN HOUR OR SO WOULD SUFFICE.
FINE BY ME! JUST TELL ME *WHEN*.
I'LL CALL AND LET YOU KNOW.
HERE'S MY *NUMBER*. THANKS, MS. RUDOLPH!
WILL! SINCE WHEN ARE YOU SO CHUMMY WITH OUR MATH TEACHER?
MS. RUDOLPH WAS SO NICE! I WAS IN A REAL BIND TODAY. I EXPECTED TO GET *AN "F"*!
...AND YOU TOTALLY WOULD HAVE, IF *SOMEONE* HADN'T SAVED YOU!
AND THAT'S NOT ALL! MS. RUDOLPH SAID SHE'D GIVE ME A *PRIVATE LESSON*!
HUH... LOOK AT THAT...
MAKING FRIENDS WITH SHEFFIELD TEACHERS MUST *RUN IN THE FAMILY*...
WHAT DO YOU MEAN, CORNELIA?

WELL...IT LOOKS LIKE YOUR MOM IS HAVING LUNCH WITH MR. COLLINS!
!
BAR
SEE YOU TOMORROW, WILL!
I...
BA
!

BAR

WILL!

GO AWAY! LEAVE ME ALONE!

THANK GOD FOR CHOCOLATE...

Are you okay, Miss Will?

YES, JAMES, I'M FINE!

Are you sure? Usually when you open that jar, it means you're sad!

WELL... TODAY I'D NEED A WHOLE **BARREL** OF CHOCOLATE, THEN!

*IT WOULDN'T HELP MUCH, THOUGH! IF ONLY I COULD HAVE A **NORMAL** FAMILY!*

*IN A **NORMAL** HOUSE, JUST LIKE MY FRIENDS! I WISH I HAD A REGULAR FAMILY, WITH PEOPLE WHO LOVE EACH OTHER...*

"...A FAMILY LIKE EVERY-BODY ELSE, WITH NO SECRETS ...
"...NO MYSTERIES...
"...NO LIES ..."
IS HAY LIN NOT COMING HOME FOR LUNCH?
SHE CALLED FIVE MINUTES AGO. SHE'S AT THE LIBRARY WITH IRMA.
SHE ALWAYS CALLS AT THE LAST MINUTE! SHE NEEDS TO LEARN THIS ISN'T A RESTAURANT!
BUT DEAR, THIS IS A RESTAURANT.
YOU KNOW WHAT I MEAN! I'M GOING TO GIVE HER A PIECE OF MY MIND WHEN SHE COMES HOME TONIGHT!
BLBLLBB GRUMBLE

WHAT WAS THAT?

IT WAS MY STOMACH, IRMA. I'M STARVING! IT'S LATE. LET'S GO HOME!

NEVER! I WANNA FIND OUT MS. RUDOLPH'S SECRETS!
SECRETS? SHE SPENT THE AFTERNOON GRADING TESTS! CAN'T YOU JUST ADMIT YOU WERE WRONG?

MAYBE, BUT I WANNA CHECK HER OUT ONE MORE TIME...I JUST GOT AN IDEA! YOU FREE TOMORROW MORNING?
WE HAVE SCHOOL IN THE MORNING!

WE'RE GONNA SPEND NEARLY TWENTY YEARS GOING TO SCHOOL. WE CAN AFFORD TO TAKE ONE DAY OFF!
YOU'RE GONNA DESTROY ME! WHEN I FLUNK OUT, I'LL KNOW WHO TO THANK!
BUT WHAT IF SHE REALLY IS A MONSTER? DON'T BE SELFISH, HAY LIN! THIS IS YOUR CHANCE TO SAVE THE WORLD!
NO, NO, NO. DON'T PUSH IT.
YOU GONNA CHANGE YOUR MIND?
FOR PETE'S SAKE! YOU KNOW WHAT?

"FINE!"

149

All clear, Hay?
Nobody around!

I DON'T KNOW ABOUT YOU, BUT I'M SWEATING!

WELL, THIS IS THE HOTTEST FALL IN TWENTY-FIVE YEARS...I HEARD IT ON TV.

DON'T PLAY DUMB! YOU KNOW WHAT I MEAN!

DON'T WORRY! WE'RE JUST GONNA POKE AROUND A LITTLE.

WHAT DO WE DO IF MS. RUDOLPH COMES BACK?

SHE WENT TO SCHOOL! SHE WON'T BE BACK FOR AT LEAST SIX HOURS!

PHONE CARD

WHAT ARE YOU DOING WITH THAT CARD? WHY AREN'T YOU USING THE KEY?

SO WE DON'T TOUCH ANYTHING! THIS WAY WE WON'T LEAVE ANY EVIDENCE.

CLACK

PHONE CARD

IT ALWAYS WORKS IN THE MOVIES. WATCH!

CLACK

CLACK

CRACK

OH NO!

YOU'RE SUCH A KLUTZ. LET ME.

YOU FIRST!
BUT...BUT... BUT...
CLACK
CLACK
CLACK

AND NOW, A GENTLE BREEZE...

...AND THE KEY IS BACK WHERE IT BELONGS!

BRILLIANT IDEA, **GENIUS**! YOU LOCKED US IN!

JUST STAY HERE! YOU'VE DONE ENOUGH ALREADY!
OKAY, I'LL STAND GUARD! HURRY UP!

I WOULD IF I KNEW WHAT I WAS LOOKING FOR... SEEMS LIKE A PERFECTLY ORDINARY HOUSE... HMM...

FIND ANYTHING?
NOPE! LET'S TRY UPSTAIRS!

TUMP
TUMP
TUMP

UH... NOTHING HERE...
I WOULDN'T EXACTLY CALL THAT WARDROBE AND CHEST ***NOTHING***!

IRMA! WH-WHAT ARE YOU DOING? YOU PROMISED WE WOULDN'T TOUCH ANYTHING!
I CHANGED MY MIND. THE TEMPTATION IS TOO GREAT! COME ON, HELP ME!

EEEEK!
AH-HA! DID YOU FIND SOMETHING?

OH NO...WE'RE GONNA GET **BUSTED**!
MS. RUDOLPH! WH-WHAT'S SHE DOING HERE? SHE WAS SUPPOSED TO BE AT SCHOOL!
IT'S YOUR FAULT!
IT'S YOUR FAULT! I TOLD YOU!
CHILL! **CHILL!** I HAVE A BACK-UP PLAN!
WHAT PLAN?
HIDE!
GLUNK
CREAK
-OOMPH-
OUCH...OUCH...OUCH... OH DEAR, MY BACK! IT'S TIME TO START USING THE HOME DELIVERY SERVICE...

There's your creature from METAMOOR—ARTHRITIS and all!
Shut up! She's making a call!

Ah, I'm so scared! Maybe she's gonna invite a few fellow monsters over for tea!
You wanna get bit? Seriously, want me to bite you? Just say the word if you wanna throw down, Hay Lin!

HELLO, WILL? THIS IS MS. RUDOLPH. ARE YOU FREE TO TALK?

OF COURSE, MA'AM! IT'S BREAK TIME. WHAT? THIS AFTERNOON? WELL... ALL RIGHT!

TODAY IS MY DAY OFF. I'LL BE WAITING FOR YOU AFTER SCHOOL, THEN.
SEE YOU IN A BIT!

EXCELLENT... THAT MEANS I HAVE SOME TIME TO RELAX!

I'LL ENJOY A NICE SNACK WHILE I READ...

HMM... THIS ONE!

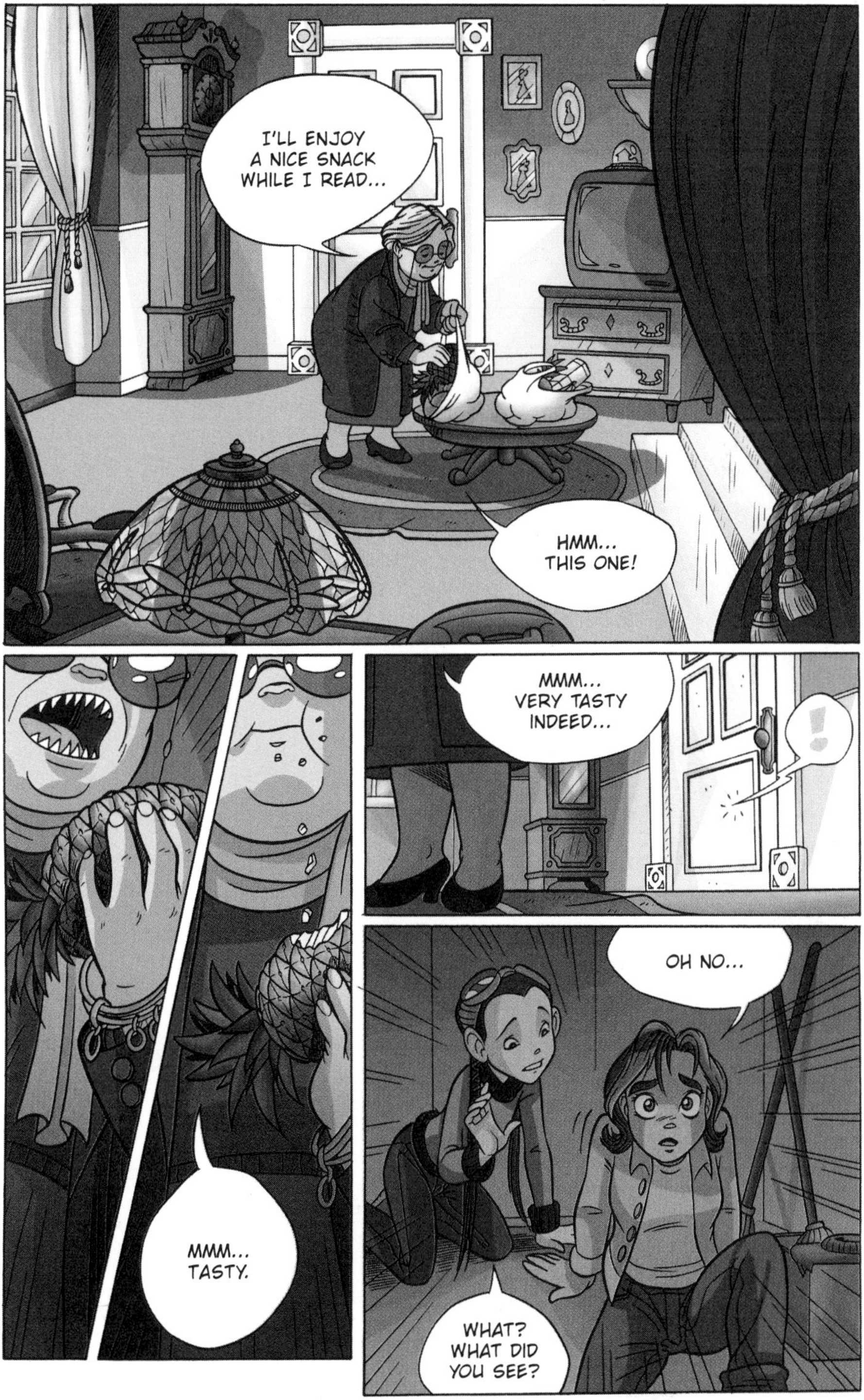

MMM... TASTY.

MMM... VERY TASTY INDEED...
!

OH NO...
WHAT? WHAT DID YOU SEE?

THESE
SHOES ARE
KILLING ME!

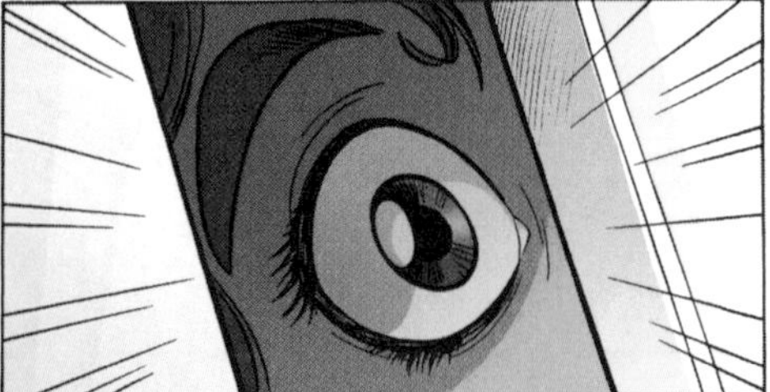

HOLD ME,
HAY LIN...
I'M GONNA...
FAINT...

BDUMP
WAKE UP, IRMA! PLEASE! OPEN YOUR EYES! *I-IRMA!*
HMM...?
EEEK!
MAY I HELP YOU, LADIES?

WILL VANDOM HAS NEVER LIKED MATH, AND MATH KNOWS THAT.

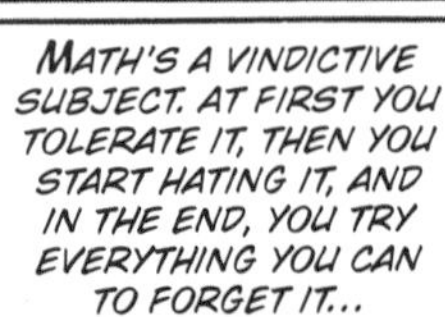

MATH'S A VINDICTIVE SUBJECT. AT FIRST YOU TOLERATE IT, THEN YOU START HATING IT, AND IN THE END, YOU TRY EVERYTHING YOU CAN TO FORGET IT...

OH, IT'S YOU, WILL!
AND BY THE TIME YOU REALIZE YOU NEED IT...
PLEASE COME IN, DEAR...

...IT'S TOO LATE!

!

BUMP

WILL! IT'S A TRAP!

MGH! MMMGH!

MS. RUDOLPH! WHAT'S GOING ON?!
I... I...

...I CAN EXPLAIN EVERYTHING, WILL!

CAREFUL, WILL! SHE'S A MONSTER FROM METAMOOR !!
UNNNH... THAT WEIRD FEELING AGAIN! SOMETHING'S IN THIS HOUSE...

...OR SOMEONE !!
WILL...

GET AWAY!
GAH!

QUICK, WILL! UNTIE US!
PLEASE, GIRLS... DON'T BE AFRAID!

THIS IS HOW I REALLY LOOK... BUT DON'T BE AFRAID! I WON'T HARM YOU!
-GASP-

YOU, WILL, ARE ***THE GUARDIAN OF THE HEART OF KANDRAKAR***...YOU'RE THE NEW GUARDIANS OF THE VEIL!
WHERE'S MS. RUDOLPH? WHAT'D YOU DO TO HER?

WAKE UP, WILL! ***SHE IS MS. RUDOLPH!***
WHY DON'T YOU UNDERSTAND? IT'S NOT WHAT IT SEEMS! YOU... YOU...

YOU SPOILED EVERYTHING!
DON'T LET HER GET AWAY!

CREAAK

WE'VE GOT HER!
SHE'S HOLED UP IN THE ATTIC!

I THOUGHT I'D NEVER PASS THROUGH THIS PORTAL AGAIN.
IT SEEMS I WAS WRONG AFTER ALL...
MS. RUDOLPH...
GOOD-BYE, GIRLS...
I'M COMING BACK... MERIDIAN!
FWOOOOOSH
IT'S A PORTAL!
WHAT DO WE DO, WILL?
THOUGHTS ARE QUICKER THAN WORDS... WILL'S ANSWER IS IN HER HAND...
...THE HEART OF KANDRAKAR KNOWS WHAT TO DO!

HEY! HURRY UP! SHE'S GETTING AWAY!
... FIRE!
FZZZZAK
LET HER GO AND FOCUS ON THE PORTAL INSTEAD!
ON MY MARK...
KZAK
KSAK
ENNNAK
FWOOOOM
PHEW...DON'T KNOW IF YOU'RE BUSY THIS AFTERNOON...
OOF...

162

"...BUT WE REALLY NEED TO HAVE A **SERIOUS** MEETING!"
PHEW...
...WHY CAN'T I STAY?
BECAUSE YOU CAN'T. THAT'S ENOUGH, LILIAN!
I BET YOU'RE TALKIN' ABOUT BOYS! I'M TELLIN' MOM!
WHAT'S UP?
WE'RE DOING OUR HOMEWORK, MOM. COULD YOU LOCK THIS LITTLE MONKEY INSIDE HER CAGE, PLEASE?
OH, THEY SQUABBLE LIKE THIS ALL THE TIME, BUT THEY LOVE EACH OTHER VERY MUCH!
SURE, MOM. AND I'LL LOVE HER EVEN MORE IF SHE STAYS AWAY FROM MY BEDROOM ALL AFTERNOON!
COME ON, LILIAN! YOUR SISTER AND HER FRIENDS HAVE TO DO THEIR HOMEWORK!
-HMPH-
WHAT WERE WE TALKING ABOUT?

TIME TO FIND OUT WHAT'S UP WITH ALL THIS!
THIS! I'VE GOT A FEELING THAT THE BOOK WE FOUND AT ELYON'S HOUSE CAN TELL US A LOT!
EVEN IF WE DON'T KNOW OUR ENEMIES, ONE THING'S FOR SURE...
...THE DENIZENS OF METAMOOR ARE AMONG US!
WE DON'T KNOW THEM, BUT THEY CLEARLY KNOW US! I'LL SAY IT AGAIN...
...LET'S KEEP OUR EYES OPEN, OKAY?
I'LL SAY IT AGAIN...I DON'T WANT TO KEEP GOING ON LIKE THIS. I WANT ANSWERS!
WHO ARE WE SUPPOSED TO BE FIGHTING? WHO ARE THOSE MONSTERS? WHAT DO THEY WANT FROM US? THE VEIL... KANDRAKAR... METAMOOR... THEY'RE JUST NAMES TO ME! AND THESE MAGICAL POWERS OF OURS...
LET'S START BY SEEING WHAT THE BOOK CAN TELL US.
IT WON'T WORK, WILL! I ALREADY TRIED OPENING IT!
THEN THIS TIME, WE'LL TRY TOGETHER!

..LET'S HOPE IT WORKS.
THIS BOOK'S PROTECTED BY A MAGIC HALO. LET'S RELEASE SOME OF OUR ENERGY AND SEE WHAT HAPPENS.
DESTROY MY BEDROOM, AND I'LL PULVERIZE YOU!
!
THAT'S RIGHT... DON'T WORRY... CAREFUL NOW...
WZZZK
THAT'S IT...
WZZZ
IT WORKED! SOMETHING'S HAPPENING!
OH!
IT'S OPENING!
DON'T... DON'T GET TOO CLOSE!
AS THE GIRLS WATCH IN SHOCK...
AH!
...THE HEAVY COVER SLOWLY OPENS, REVEALING WHAT'S INSIDE...

LOOK AT THAT... IT'S NOT REALLY A BOOK!
WHAT IS THAT?

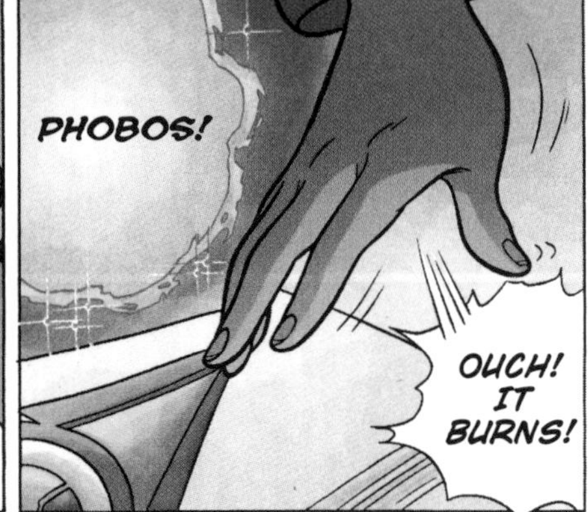

UH-OH... DID I DO SOMETHING WRONG?
I KNEW IT! I KNEW IT!
FWAMP
DUCK!
EEEK!
WOOOSH
THE DOOR'S LOCKED! WE'RE TRAPPED!
WHAT'S THAT?
YIKES! I NEVER THOUGHT I'D MISS THOSE BORING AFTERNOONS SPENT DOING MY HOMEWORK!
BUMP
BUMP
TUMP
AHH! EEEK!
THEY'RE S'POSED TO BE DOING HOMEWORK! CAN'T YOU HEAR THEM PLAYING?! CAN I GO PLAY WITH THEM?
NO, LILIAN, YOU CAN'T. THEY'RE OLDER THAN YOU. YOU'D JUST GET BORED!

AHHH!
WILL!
HEART OF KANDRAKAR... WE'RE IN DANGER!
HELP US...

168

KANDRAKAR'S LIGHT AND METAMOOR'S DARKNESS SOUNDLESSLY COLLIDE...
...AND THE HEART PREVAILS ONCE AGAIN.
BZZZ-ZZAP
CREEEAK
I BET YOU WERE TALKIN' ABOUT BOYS!
UH...
GROAN

"PHEW...
WE MADE IT AGAIN."
I CAN'T EXPLAIN IT, BUT I'M SURE...
...THERE'S A LINK BETWEEN ELYON'S HOUSE AND METAMOOR! WHAT WE DON'T KNOW IS IF THERE'S A LINK BETWEEN METAMOOR AND ELYON'S FAMILY TOO!
THAT BOOK DOESN'T PROVE ANYTHING! IT COULD'VE BEEN IN THAT CELLAR FOR AGES...
RIGHT! MAYBE ELYON AND HER PARENTS WERE UNLUCKY ENOUGH...

...TO LIVE IN A HAUNTED HOUSE—LIKE THE ONES YOU SEE IN MOVIES!
I THINK THE WHOLE TOWN IS HAUNTED!

ONE PORTAL IN THE GYM, ANOTHER IN ELYON'S HOUSE, AND A THIRD IN MS. RUDOLPH'S ATTIC!

170

AND THERE ARE NINE MORE...
OH, YOU'RE RIGHT... WE WERE FORGETTING YOUR AMAZING MAP...
Heatherfield
THE WORLD'S MOST USELESS MAP! THE ONLY ONE THAT SHOWS YOU SOMETHING AFTER YOU FIND IT!

MY GRANDMA MUST'VE GIVEN THIS TO ME FOR A REASON—OR MAYBE YOU KNOW BEST PER USUAL, IRMA SHERLOCK?!
GULP

LOOK! THE HEART OF KANDRAKAR'S POINTING AT SOMETHING...

THAT'S ELYON'S HOUSE!

THAT'S A PRETTY CLEAR MESSAGE...

SHORTLY...

THIS PLACE GIVES ME THE SHIVERS!

I DON'T LIKE IT EITHER, BUT IT'S THE ONLY CLUE WE HAVE TO FIND OUT WHAT HAPPENED TO ELYON!

HERE WE ARE... NOW WHAT?
THERE MUST BE A REASON THE HEART OF KANDRAKAR LED US HERE...

PHOBOS... PHOBOS...
LISTEN! LISTEN!

WE... WE CAN'T HEAR ANYTHING, TARANEE!
IT'S THAT SAME VOICE! IT'S WHISPERING A NAME... PHOBOS!

WHAT NOW? THE SEAL'S LOCKED INSIDE THE HEART.
AND IT SHOULD STAY THERE!

THE HEART OF KANDRAKAR ALWAYS KNOWS WHAT'S RIGHT...
FORGET THAT! I DON'T WANT THAT THING TELLING ME WHAT TO DO!

SURE, IT SAVED US ONCE, BUT THERE'S NO GUARANTEE IT WILL EVERY TIME! IT COULD... I MEAN, ITS BATTERY MIGHT DIE!
Can I turn her into a crow?
Nobody'd notice the difference...

I HEARD THAT! WHY DON'T YOU SAY IT TO MY FACE?
ER, UH...
HAH! NOT LAUGHING NOW, ARE YOU? YOU'RE SCARED OF ME!
I-IT'S NOT YOU I'M SCARED OF...
AH!
...IT'S WHAT'S BEHIND YOU!
THE PORTAL! IT'S OPEN AGAIN!
I THINK I GOT IT! THE SEAL OF PHOBOS IS THE KEY TO ENTER METAMOOR!
WOW!
ARE YOU THINKING WHAT I'M THINKING?
KANDRAKAR THE FORTRESS OF THE CONGREGATION.
OUT OF THE WAY! LET ME THROUGH...

...I MUST SPEAK TO THE ORACLE!
NOW IS NOT THE TIME.
THE ORACLE CAN'T SEE YOU RIGHT NOW!
THAT REMAINS TO BE SEEN!
STOP!
SIR...
LET HER IN, TIBOR! I KNOW LUBA'S THOUGHTS... AND LUBA ALREADY KNOWS MY ANSWER!
THIS MUST NOT BE, ORACLE! THE GUARDIANS AREN'T READY YET! THEY'RE TOO INEXPERIENCED!
WHAT YOU SAY IS TRUE... BUT IT MUST BE. EVEN I CAN'T CHANGE THAT!
THAT'S A LIE! YOU CAN STOP THEM IF YOU WISH!
WHAT GALL!
SHOULD THEY FAIL, THE VEIL WILL BE EXPOSED TO PHOBOS'S ATTACKS...
THOSE GIRLS ARE BRAVE, LUBA! HAVE FAITH IN THEM...
TEN THOUSAND YEARS AGO, YOU WERE ONCE THAT YOUNG.

OKAY...
...WE CAN GO NOW!

ARE WE SUPPOSED TO JUMP INTO THAT **RING OF FIRE**?
FORGET IT! I'M NO **CIRCUS CLOWN**!
WOOOOOSH
THOSE DEFINITELY AREN'T NORMAL FLAMES...
... BUT MAYBE YOUR POWERS WILL WORK ON THEM ANYWAY, TARANEE.
WE'LL FIND OUT IN A SECOND!
DID YOU HEAR ME?
GET OUTTA THE WAY!
WOW! THEY DID WHAT I TOLD THEM!
COME ON, LET'S GO!
WAIT A MINUTE! WHAT IF WE GET STUCK ON THE OTHER SIDE?
WAMPH
WE HAVE THE SEAL OF PHOBOS! IF IT GOT US IN, IT'LL GET US OUT.
OH! SO WHO'S **MISS KNOW-IT-ALL** NOW, HUH? YOU ACT LIKE YOU'VE BEEN DOING THIS STUFF **YOUR WHOLE LIFE**!
YOU'RE RIGHT, CORNELIA... BUT SOMETHING TELLS ME IT'LL WORK!

AND MAYBE ELYON'S ON THE OTHER SIDE! THAT'S A GOOD ENOUGH REASON TO GO!

RIGHT! WHO'S COMING WITH ME?

BUT... BUT WE'RE IN HEATHER-FIELD!
GEE! WE WENT THE WRONG WAY!
THAT'S REALLY WEIRD— NOBODY'S AROUND. AND LISTEN... NO NOISE!
OH! SOMEBODY'S OVER THERE!
SIR! PLEASE, SIR! DON'T RUN AWAY! WAIT!
SIR! PLEASE OPEN THE DOOR! I JUST WANT TO...
BAM
BAM
KRRRRR
... TALK TO YOU! GASP
WHAT DID YOU DO?
DON'T LOOK AT ME! IT'S NOT MY FAULT!

EEEEK!
WHOA! I THINK IT'S CLEAR...
...THIS *DEFINITELY* ISN'T *HEATHERFIELD!*
!

WELCOME, GUARDIANS! WE'VE BEEN WAITING FOR YOU A LONG TIME...

I DIDN'T COME ALONE...
...AND WE EVEN PREPARED A WELCOMING COMMITTEE!

SAY HELLO TO YOUR FRIENDS, ELYON!

ELYON! WH-WHAT DID THEY DO TO YOU?
NOTHING! I'M FINE. I'M SO HAPPY TO SEE YOU GUYS!

WE'RE GOING HOME, AND YOU'RE COMING WITH US! YOU CAN'T STAY IN THIS HORRIBLE PLACE!
HA-HA! YOU DON'T UNDER-STAND...

...THIS "HORRIBLE PLACE" HAS A NAME, YOU KNOW! WELCOME TO MERIDIAN, MY FRIENDS ...
...WELCOME TO MY HOME!

STAY! YOU'LL LIKE IT!
SURE! MAYBE I'LL ASK MY PARENTS TO RENT A COTTAGE HERE FOR SUMMER BREAK!

DON'T YOU WANT TO STAY? I'M SO SORRY...
YOU LEAVE US WITH NO CHOICE...

GUARDS! TAKE THEM!
I KNEW HE WAS GONNA SAY THAT! *I KNEW!*

DON'T LET THEM GET CLOSE!
BZZZ
BZZZAP

WOOOSHH
RAAAAARGH!
POW!
OH! NEVER, EVER HIT A WOMAN...
...LET ALONE ONE WITH A RED-HOT SWORD!
FSSSS
YEOW!

CR-A-A-CK-K

DON'T STOP NOW! IT'S WORKING!

UGH!

THIS'D BE FUN IF I WASN'T TERRIFIED!

YOU WERE ALMOST IN! DON'T DISAPPOINT MY FRIEND!

HEY, HEY, HEY...

BUMP

I THINK YOU OWE ME A FAVOR.

WHAT WOULD I DO WITHOUT YOU?

THEY'RE TOO STRONG FOR OUR SOLDIERS, SIR!

QUICK! LET'S GET OUT OF HERE BEFORE MORE SOLDIERS ARRIVE!

CURSES! DON'T LET THEM GET AWAY!

CALL FROST THE HUNTER! YOUR STUPID GUARDS WILL BE PUNISHED FOR THEIR INCOMPETENCE...

I WON'T LET YOU DOWN, LORD CEDRIC...

...NO ONE ESCAPES FROST!
SNORT
YAAAAH!
TAPADUMP

WHERE SHOULD WE GO? LET'S STOP A MINUTE AND USE OUR HEADS!
THAT WAY! LET'S HIDE IN THERE!

GET INSIDE, QUICK! SOMEONE'S COMING!

TADADUMP TADADUMP

RRRRRH...

STOP, CRIMSON...

What's going on?

Nothing you'd like, I'm afraid! Hold your breath and don't move...

THAT MEANS ME TOO?

-GULP- WE'RE NOT ALONE!

Shhhh! There's a brute on a red horse out there, and he looks really mad!
-GASP- HE'S... F-FROST THE HUNTER!

FORGIVE ME, FROST! I'VE GOT NOTHING TO DO WITH IT! THEY JUST RAN INSIDE!
I COULDN'T STOP THEM!
!

INSIDE THE SHED, YOU SAY? MY INSTINCTS WERE RIGHT...

CAN YOU HEAR ME, GIRLS? ARE YOU COMING OUT ON YOUR OWN, OR SHALL I COME FETCH YOU?
I DON'T LIKE EITHER OF THOSE OPTIONS! ANY IDEAS?
THAT GIANT ISN'T JUST GONNA GIVE UP! HE WANTS *US*!
WE'D NEED BAIT! SOMETHING TO DISTRACT HIM WHILE WE ESCAPE!
THEN THAT'S WHAT HE'LL GET! WE'LL USE THE HEART OF KANDRAKAR TO CREATE A MIRAGE...
...THAT LOOKS LIKE US...
THAT'S NOT ALADDIN'S LAMP!
...AND I DO BELIEVE.
IT CAN IF YOU BELIEVE, CORNELIA ...
FOR IMDHAL'S LIGHTNING!

YOU'RE FAST, GUARDIANS, BUT MY SWORD IS FASTER!
SLAM
C-C-CRACK
EH? WHAT SORCERY IS THIS?
Now's our chance! Let's go!
WHIIINNY!
GAH!
YOUR LITTLE TRICK DIDN'T WORK! YOU ARE MINE!
WELL DONE, FROST! WHERE ARE THE OTHERS?
YOU'LL SOON HAVE THEM! CAN YOU HEAR ME, GIRLS?
COME FOR YOUR FRIEND...
...AND I WON'T HARM A HAIR ON HER HEAD!
LET ME THINK! LET ME THINK!
WILL!

DON'T LISTEN TO HIM! **RUN!**

NO, TARANEE...

...YOU SHOULDN'T HAVE DONE THAT!

WHOOSH

WHAT A VIPER! CAN YOU BELIEVE WHAT SHE DID?!
I SAY WE GO TEACH 'EM A LESSON!

NO! RUN AWAY— PLEASE, GO! RUN AWAY! LISTEN TO ME, WILL...

RUN AWAY!
I CAN HEAR TARANEE'S THOUGHTS...

HEART OF KANDRAKAR... TAKE US HOME!
BUT WILL...

DROP IT AND JUST DO AS I SAY!

EPILOGUE...
WOOOOSHHHHHH
LET'S CONCENTRATE...
WHY ARE YOU STARING?
IS SOMETHING WRONG WITH ME?
GEE... LOOKS LIKE TARANEE...SOUNDS LIKE TARANEE...BUT IT'S NOT TARANEE!
WE'VE GOT NO CHOICE! IF TARANEE DOESN'T GO HOME TONIGHT, WE'LL BE IN DEEP TROUBLE!
WE HAD A CHOICE...
SHE TOLD ME TO GO, CORNELIA, BUT WE'RE GOING BACK. IF IT'S THE LAST THING WE DO, WE'LL RESCUE HER FROM MERIDIAN!
WILL ALWAYS KEEPS HER WORD.
END OF CHAPTER 3

4

THE POWER OF FIRE
"What if you were replaced by an astral drop...?"

A SMILE.

TARANEE SMILES, AND HAY LIN CAN'T HELP BUT STARE.

SETTLE DOWN, GUYS! LET'S CALL THE ROLL!

IT HAD BEEN LIKE A DREAM. DISCOVERING THEIR MAGIC POWERS, HER GRANDMA'S DISAPPEARANCE, THE TRIP TO METAMOOR...

BENSON!

HERE!

AND THEN HER VOICE AGAIN...

IF HAY LIN HADN'T SEEN HER FRIEND IMPRISONED, SHE'D HAVE SWORN THAT WAS HER—**RIGHT THERE.**

BUT THE **REAL TARANEE** WAS REPLACED BY A PERFECT DOUBLE. AND THIS WAS NO DREAM...

LIN!

?

YOU ARE HAY LIN, AREN'T YOU?
OF COURSE! WHO ELSE HAS THAT NAME! I'M UNIQUE! THE ONE AND ONLY!
PRESENZE
IRREPLACEABLE...
OKAY, 'COS I'M THE UNIQUE MATH **ASSISTANT** WHO'S GONNA BE WITH YOU FOR A LONG TIME!
MISS **RUDOLPH,** YOUR TEACHER, IS ABSENT, AND I HAVE TO FIND OUT HOW PROFICIENT YOU ARE IN HER CLASS.
PRESENZE
THAT'S WHY WE'RE GOING TO BE HAVING A QUIZ!
12
13
IRMA! What's up? Aren't you ready?
When was I ever? I was just thinking that math was her favorite subject...
...TARANEE'S...
12
13

TARANEE! WE'RE HERE!
MY PARENTS ARE CALLING! TODAY'S THEIR ANNIVERSARY, AND WE'RE GOING OUT FOR LUNCH. SEE YOU LATER!
HAVE FUN!
AND TRY NOT TO OVERDO IT!
CORNELIA, DON'T TREAT HER LIKE THAT! SHE HAS TO SEEM LIKE TARANEE IN EVERY WAY.
WHATEVER! BUT DON'T FORGET THAT WE'RE THE ONES WHO MADE HER USING MAGIC, WILL!
THAT ISN'T TARANEE. IT'S A...A...
AN ASTRAL DROP!
PLUS, SHE'S LIKE OUR FRIEND BUT AS A DROP OF WATER. COME ON, LOOK! WATCH HER WITH HER FAMILY...
ASTRAL DROP? BEAUTIFUL NAME!
SO CLEVER! DON'T YOU HAVE ANYTHING BETTER TO DO, HAY LIN?
I LIKE IT!

193

THEY SMILE, TOUCH HER...

I WONDER...
IF AN ASTRAL DROP
TOOK MY PLACE, WOULD
MY MOM REALIZE?
NO!
NO WAY!
WILL!
WANNA GET
A MOVE ON?
THE BUS
AWAITS.
COMING!

HEY! IT'S ALREADY HERE! WANT ME TO POP ITS TIRES TO SLOW IT DOWN?
IT'S PROBABLY BETTER IF YOU DON'T USE MAGIC. YOU WANT THE BUS DRIVER TO PEEL AWAY?
85 STATION
BUS

IRMA, YOU'RE NOT REMOTELY FUNNY!
IF I WANTED YOU TO LAUGH, I'D DRESS LIKE A CLOWN!
SSSSSH

THAT WOULD BE DIFFERENT FROM WHAT YOU'RE WEARING NOW HOW?
HELP! WHO'S GOT THE ANTIVENOM?
COME ON, CORNELIA, THIS IS NO TIME TO FIGHT.

YOU'RE THE LAST ONE WHO'LL GET ME TO SHUT UP, WILL!
WHAT'S THAT SUPPOSED TO MEAN?

IF IT WASN'T FOR YOU, RIGHT NOW...
YEAH? KEEP GOING!

IF IT WASN'T FOR ME, TARANEE'D BE WITH US, RIGHT? ***RIGHT?***
NO...NO, THAT'S NOT WHAT I MEANT!

BUT IT'S WHAT YOU ***THOUGHT***!
CALM DOWN, WILL. WE'RE ALL EXHAUSTED. LET'S GET OFF AT THE NEXT STOP.

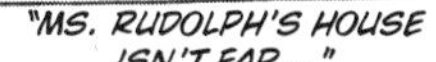
"MS. RUDOLPH'S HOUSE ISN'T FAR..."

SO?
NOTHING! THE PORTAL WON'T OPEN!

AND THE SEAL OF PHOBOS DOESN'T GIVE ANY SIGNS OF LIFE!
THAT'LL HELP US LEAVE METAMOOR, BUT GETTING IN'S A DIFFERENT STORY.
WE CAN'T LEAVE TARANEE! WE'LL FIND A PORTAL THAT'S ALREADY OPEN! AGREED?
NO DISCUSSION NEEDED! HAY LIN, HAVE YOU GOT THE MAP OF THE PORTALS ?

YEAH, BUT YOU TAKE IT. I... GOTTA GO.
?

What's up with her?
Dunno... She's been acting weird since we got here.

LOOK! THE HEART OF KANDRAKAR...

...IT'S SHOWING US THE WAY!

THE AIR,
MY ELEMENT...
HE'S CALLING
ME ...

A MUSIC
BOX!

STRANGE...I'VE NEVER HEARD IT BEFORE, BUT THIS MUSIC REMINDS ME OF SOMETHING...
"SOMETHING!

"SOMEONE..."

AH!
CRUNCK

HAY LIN! EVERYTHING ALL RIGHT?
I...THINK SO, YEAH... THIS MUSIC REMINDS ME OF SOME-THING!
SO? LOTS OF SONGS DREDGE UP MEMORIES.
YEAH, BUT... THIS MEMORY **WASNT MINE**!
I'VE WATCHED CREATURES ENTER THE PORTAL IN THIS ATTIC AND HAD A CLEAR FEELING OF... **FEAR**!
THEN I SAW THAT **LITTLE GIRL'S** FACE AND KNEW IT!
MAYBE YOU'VE DISCOVERED A NEW POWER, HAY LIN!
YOU MEAN SHE SEES OTHER PEOPLE'S MEMORIES WHEN SHE HEARS MUSIC THEY LIKE?
YES! AND THAT MEMORY COULD BE MS. RUDOLPH'S!
YEAH! SHE'S FROM META-MOOR, AND HAY LIN SAW HER MEMORY OF WHEN SHE CAME TO EARTH!
IF WHAT YOU'RE SAYING IS TRUE, THEN I WONDER...
...WHY WAS SHE SO SCARED? AND WHAT WAS SHE RUNNING FROM?

IN THE LAIRS' GARDEN...

WHAT EXCUSE DIDJA MAKE UP TO GO TO MS. RUDOLPH'S?
I SAID WE WERE EATING AT YOUR PARENTS' RESTAURANT, SO BACK ME UP.

TROUBLE IS, NOW I'M HUNGRY! THINK I'LL STOP BY MY FRIDGE BEFORE I LEAVE!

SEE YA LATER AT YOU-KNOW-WHERE! AND WEAR SOMETHING APPROPRIATE!
GOTCHA!

HOPE MOM DOESN'T BUST ME...

201

WHERE HAVE YOU BEEN?

I CALLED HAY LIN'S RESTAURANT, AND THEY SAID YOU WEREN'T THERE!
TAKEOUT, MOM! WE GRABBED IT AND ATE AT WILL'S.

DON'T RUN OFF, MISS QUICK-ANSWER! YOU HAVE A SURPRISE IN THE SITTING ROOM!
AH, REALLY? A LIGHT SNACK?

HI, LITTLE BISCUIT!
NO, HE'S SOMETHING HEAVY!

MARTIN! WHY ARE YOU DRESSED LIKE THAT, AND HOW'D YOU GET IN HERE?
I'M AN EXPLORER SCOUT IN THE HEATHERFIELD HAPPY BEARS, AND YOUR DAD OPENED THE DOOR!
GOTTA GO NOW... MY SHIFT STARTS IN HALF AN HOUR!

I BROUGHT YOU A CALENDAR! I USUALLY SELL 'EM, BUT FOR YOU, IT'S A GIFT!
LOOK! THIS MONTH, THERE'S A PICTURE OF TWO LOVE-BIRDS!

SPIT IT OUT, MARTIN! WHADDAYA WANT FOR IT?
TONIGHT, THE LITTLE BEARS ARE LOOKING AT THE SLIDES! WANNA JOIN US?

RELAX, IRMA! TAKE A DEEP BREATH AND...
NO THANK YOU!

IT'S A LOTTA FUN! PLUS, WE HAVE A BAND AND...
YEAH—THE HAPPY PLANTIGRADES! GOOD-BYE, MARTIN!

"NO THANKS!" SHE HAD TO SAY THAT 'COS HER PARENTS WERE THERE! BUT THE HAPPY PLANTIGRADES ISN'T A BAD NAME...
CLUD

THE UNIFORM USED TO BE MORE FLATTERING...LOOK AT ME AND YOUR MOTHER!
YOU MEAN A FEW WAIST SIZES BACK, RIGHT?

"THIS MONTH THERE'S A PICTURE OF TWO LOVEBIRDS," HUH?
UH-OH! STRATEGIC WITHDRAWAL!

SO LONG, SIS! NOW LET'S SEE IF YOU CAN...
CLACK

AAAH! DADDY! MOMMY!
TAKE THAT!

WHAT'S HAPPENING, CHRISTOPHER?
WATER'S FLOODIN' OUTTA THE SHOWER! I'M GETTIN' SOAKED!
SSSSHHH

NEARBY, ANOTHER SORT OF MAGIC...

A KISS! IS THAT ASKING SO MUCH?

AAAH!
IT'S MATT!
FRUUSH

HE WAS HOME! WHY DIDN'T I THINK OF THAT? DID HE SEE ME?
AH! HERE YOU ARE, DORMOUSE!

WHERE'S YOUR MASTER?
PHEEW! NEXT TIME, I'LL WRITE A NOTE! TEXTS ARE TOO FAST!

LOOK AT HOW HE'S PETTING IT! WHY CAN'T I BE A DORMOUSE?
-SIGH-

DID YOU HEAR SOMETHING?
OOPS!

WELP, GOTTA TEND THE GARDEN! NO TELLING WHAT KINDA BUGS ARE INFESTING THAT NETTLE BUSH.
BUGS? NETTLES?

A CLIFF EAST OF HEATHERFIELD. SHELL CAVE. 5:00 P.M.

WHERE'S WILL? IT'S COLD OUT HERE!

SHE CALLED SAYING SHE'D BE LATE. SHE HAD TO TAKE A SHOWER.

SINCE YOU'RE NEW IN TOWN, ALLOW ME TO INTRODUCE YOU TO SHELL CAVE!
IT'S DEFINITELY GOT CHARACTER...

WHAT'S UP? WHY ARE YOU SCRATCHING LIKE THAT, WILL?
BECAUSE NETTLES HAVE HATEFUL, *ITCHY* LEAVES!

THAT'S NOT AN ANSWER.
THE SAD FACT IS I'M ALLERGIC TO NETTLES, BUT I'LL FILL YOU IN LATER...
LET'S GET TO WORK, GIRLS!

WE NEED TO START BY CREATING **ASTRAL DROPS** TO TAKE OUR PLACE!
IS THAT REALLY NECESSARY?
WE DON'T KNOW WHEN WE'LL BE BACK! HECK, WE DON'T EVEN KNOW IF WE'LL...
WE'RE ***DEFINITELY*** COMING BACK, CORNELIA—WITH TARANEE!

IF YOU'RE SO SURE, WHY AREN'T YOU FOCUSING TOO?
PIPE DOWN, AND I WILL!
I'M DOING THIS FOR YOU, TARANEE!
JUST FOR YOU!

INCREDIBLE! YOU'RE... ***ME***?
HEY! PINCH YER OWN NOSE!

I DON'T KNOW ABOUT YOU, BUT I THINK I LOOK GOOD!
I'M SEEING DOUBLE!

FANTASTIC! IT'S LIKE LOOKING AT OUR REFLECTIONS IN A MIRROR!

I SURE HOPE NOT! I DON'T HAVE ***SPLIT ENDS***!

WHAT'D YOU SAY?
OH YEAH. THEY REALLY ARE LIKE US!

UM...MAYBE NOT ALL OF THEM...
?

I LIVE ON... WHAT STREET DO I LIVE ON? HMM...

TABULA RASA! COMPLETELY EMPTY! ZERO POINTS!
UNLIKE OURS, YOUR ASTRAL DROP DOESN'T SEEM TO REMEMBER ANYTHING...

WELL...WHEN I WAS CREATING HER, I THOUGHT MAYBE SHE COULD...
TAKE YOUR PLACE FOR GOOD?

SO WHAT IF IT'S A BAD COPY? LET'S JUST MAKE ANOTHER!
NO. THERE'S NO GUARANTEE IT WON'T HAPPEN AGAIN.

CORNELIA'S RIGHT. IT'S MY FAULT, AND I KNOW HOW TO FIX IT!
LOOK, I'M WRITING DOWN EVERYTHING YOU SHOULD AND SHOULDN'T DO HERE. YOU CAN READ, RIGHT, WILL?
SURE, SURE! JUST ONE QUESTION...
WHO'S THIS "WILL"?

STILL HEATHERFIELD'S CLIFF. SHELL CAVE. 7:30 P.M.
YOUR ASTRAL DROP LEFT TOO, HAY LIN?
YEAH! I REALLY GRILLED HER. SEEMS LIKE SHE KNOWS EVERYTHING.
SHE'LL GO HOME, LIE DOWN IN MY BED, AND HAVE **MY** DREAMS!
MEANWHILE, WE'RE HEADING INTO A WORLD OF **NIGHTMARES**!

AGAIN—ONE MORE TIME!
WAKE UP AT 7:00, **SHOWER** AT A QUARTER PAST 7:00, GIVE MOM A **KISS** AT TEN TO 8:00, BREAKFAST AT...

OKAY, OKAY...IF YOU FOLLOW THE INSTRUCTIONS, YOU CAN'T GO WRONG! AND REMEMBER...
...STUDY WHAT I SHOULDN'T DO! I GOT IT! YOU WROTE IT IN **BLACK**!

-SIGH- I HOPE SHE AT LEAST FINDS THE HOUSE...
IT'S DO OR DIE TIME, WILL—HURRY UP!

IT'S DARK! LUCKILY, HAY LIN AND ME BROUGHT EQUIPMENT!
I'VE BEEN TO THIS CAVE THOUSANDS OF TIMES AND NEVER IMAGINED I'D FIND A **PORTAL**!

SO MUCH GRAFFITI... I NEVER NOTICED BEFORE.

I LOVE ANNE S.R.

ANNE + BILLY

SORRY, S.R.

JONAS WAS HERE

SHE GOES OUT WITH HIM ONE SUMMER... BUT DATES SOMEBODY ELSE AT THE SAME TIME...

EVERY CARVING'S A TESTIMONY OF LOVE... THIS IS HISTORY, MY DEARS!
WRONG, IRMA. IT'S JUST ***VANDALISM***!

NOW THAT I HAVE THE POWER OF THE ***EARTH***, I REALIZE MORE AND MORE THAT PEOPLE...

...DON'T RESPECT IT!
HEY! LOOK HERE!

THIS DRAWING'S SO FAR FROM THE REST!
A BLUE FIRE WITH FOUR FLAMES! SO WHAT?

IT'S THE SAME ONE IRMA SKETCHED IN HER DIARY THIS MORNING!
NO WAY! I HAVEN'T BEEN HERE FOR A YEAR AND WAS TOTALLY DAYDREAMING WHEN I DREW IT!

IT'S OKAY, GIRLS... JUST FEELING FAINT...
...LIKE YOU DO WHENEVER YOU'RE **NEAR A PORTAL**! MAYBE THIS IS IT!

YOU KNOW PERFECTLY WELL SHE ASKED ME ***TO LEAVE*** HER IN METAMOOR! SHE DID IT TO SAVE US!
I'M NOT QUESTIONING THAT, BUT I'D HAVE LIKED TO HEAR HER SAY IT TOO!
MIRIAM LARRY
YOU DON'T GET IT, DO YOU?! YOU'RE LUCKY NOT HEARING HER DESPERATE CRY ***EXPLODE IN YOUR HEAD*** EVERY HOUR! EVERY MINUTE...
...EVERY SECOND...
WILL...
SHHHH!
GUYS— LISTEN!
WHAT? I DON'T HEAR ANYTHING.
THAT'S THE POINT! WHAT HAPPENED TO THE NOISE FROM THE ***WAVES*** AND THE SEA?

AND THAT'S NOT ALL! THERE'S AN ODD WHITE LIGHT, AND THE WALLS OF THE CAVE GOT ALL... *SMOOTH*!

WOOOOO
BUT WHAT...?
ALMOST LIKE A *REAL* SHELL!

WATER! SO MUCH WATER!
IRMA! DO SOMETHING!
WOOOSH

MAYBE I CAN MAKE...

...AN AIR BUBBLE!

OKAY, THERE'S NO WAY THAT WAVE WAS AN ***ANOMALY!*** WE'VE CROSSED THE PORTAL!
QUICK, PUT THESE ON!

...TO NOTHING!
EEEK!
I-IRMA! YOUR "NOTHING"...
...IS STARING AT US!
BUMP

...AND IT SEEMS QUITE CURIOUS.
MOM! COME LOOK!
I CAN'T RIGHT NOW, FARGART!

BUT THE HERMIT CRAB I FOUND AT THE MARKET'S LEAVING ITS LITTLE HOUSE!
THAT WAS JUST AN EMPTY SHELL! STOP PICKING UP THINGS FROM THE GROUND!

I DIDN'T PICK IT UP! I FOUND IT!
I'VE GOT A BAD FEELING ABOUT THIS, GIRLS!

IF I'VE GOT THIS STRAIGHT, WE'RE IN METAMOOR, BUT WE'RE REALLY, REALLY TINY, RIGHT?
RIGHT! AND WE'RE FLOATING IN SOME KINDA GLASS BOWL!

THE PROBLEM IS, I ONLY KNOW ONE THING PEOPLE USE GLASS BOWLS FOR!
A-ARE YOU SAYING... A GOLDFISH COULD BE WAITING FOR ITS LUNCH OUT THERE?

AAAH!
THAT'S WORSE!

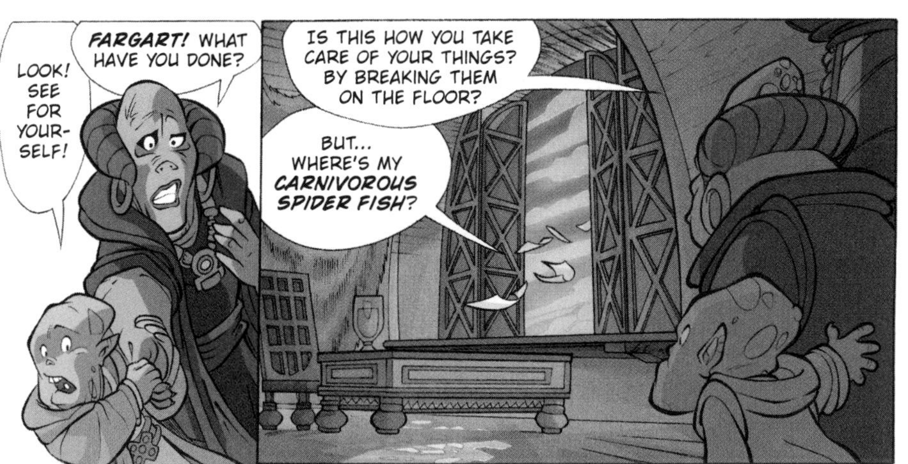
LOOK! SEE FOR YOURSELF!
FARGART! WHAT HAVE YOU DONE?
IS THIS HOW YOU TAKE CARE OF YOUR THINGS? BY BREAKING THEM ON THE FLOOR?
BUT... WHERE'S MY **CARNIVOROUS SPIDER FISH**?

HERE IT IS, POOR THING... LOOK HOW IT'S TREMBLING—IT'S TERRIFIED!

I...I DON'T UNDERSTAND!
WE'LL DISCUSS THIS WHEN YOUR FATHER GETS HOME!

MAN, I LOVE OUR POWERS! WE'RE BACK TO THE RIGHT SIZE.
AND NOT A MOMENT TOO SOON!

WE MADE IT! TARANEE'S GOTTA BE HERE SOMEWHERE!
GOTTA TELL YA, WILL—I'DA BEEN HAPPIER NEVER SEEING THIS PLACE AGAIN.

HAY LIN, WHAT'S UP WITH YOU?
NOTHING, CORNELIA. THE AIR IN MERIDIAN'S ALLEYS IS TALKING TO ME...
I HEAR THE VOICES, SMELL THE PERFUMES... THESE MONSTERS AREN'T SO DIFFERENT FROM US...
LAST TIME WE WERE HERE, I FELT LIKE AN OUTSIDER, BUT TODAY...
...TODAY, IT FRIGHTENS ME LESS!

SILENCE REIGNS IN KANDRAKAR, IN THE EXACT CENTER OF INFINITY.

THE CONGREGATION HAS ENDED. THE WISE MEN HAVE DEPARTED. IT IS TIME FOR THE ORACLE TO MEDITATE...

...AND TO DECIDE...

SPEAK TO ME, ORACLE. ALLOW ME TO BE THE LIGHT THAT DISPELS THE CLOUD TROUBLING YOU.

GOOD TIBOR, I'LL SHARE MY CONCERNS.

THE **CHOSEN ONES** HAVE BROKEN THE LAWS OF KANDRAKAR ONCE MORE. OBSERVE.

I DON'T UNDERSTAND. THEY ARE MERELY GOING ABOUT THEIR DAYS...

WHAT YOU SEE ARE **MAGICAL CONSTRUCTS**. THEY CALL THEM... **ASTRAL DROPS**!

PERFECT COPIES! HOW DID THEY BECOME SUCH SKILLED PRACTIONERS OF THEIR ART?

THERE IS NOTHING ADMIRABLE ABOUT IT. THEIR TASK IS CLOSING PORTALS, NOT CROSSING THEM.

MUST YOU PUNISH THEM?
THIS IS WHAT I MUST WEIGH. THEY NOW TRESPASS IN THE LANDS OF PRINCE PHOBOS!

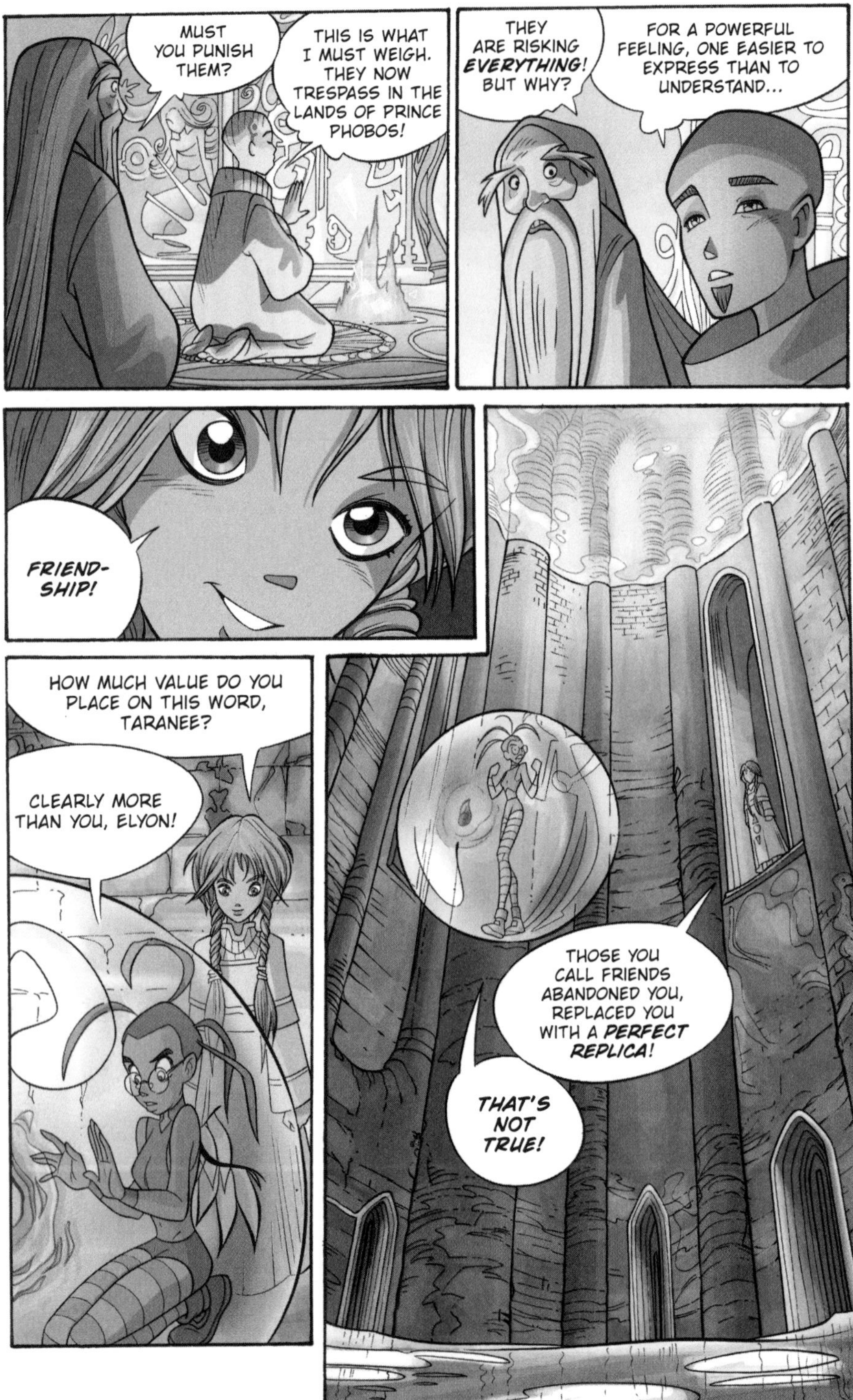

THEY ARE RISKING **EVERYTHING**! BUT WHY?
FOR A POWERFUL FEELING, ONE EASIER TO EXPRESS THAN TO UNDERSTAND...

FRIENDSHIP!

HOW MUCH VALUE DO YOU PLACE ON THIS WORD, TARANEE?
CLEARLY MORE THAN YOU, ELYON!

THOSE YOU CALL FRIENDS ABANDONED YOU, REPLACED YOU WITH A ***PERFECT REPLICA***!

THAT'S NOT TRUE!

YOU'VE ALREADY SEEN THE REFLECTION IN THE **WELL OF APPEARANCE**! THAT IS YOU!
I'VE HAD ENOUGH OF YOUR MAGICAL TRICKS! WHY ARE YOU DOING THIS TO ME? **WHY?**

I WAS WONDERING MUCH THE SAME... MAY WE SPEAK?

CEDRIC!

I THOUGHT YOU DIDN'T WANT THE GUARDIANS TO SEE YOUR HUMAN FORM!
INDEED. DON'T WORRY, TARANEE DIDN'T SEE ME. SHALL WE DISCUSS HER?

SHE'S THE WEAKEST AMONG THE GUARDIANS, AND I'M PRETTY SURE I CAN BRING HER TO **OUR** SIDE!
DO AS YOU LIKE, BUT BE VERY CAREFUL.

THE **CAGE** EXISTS **SYMBIOTICALLY** WITH ITS PRISONER.
I KNOW, BUT TARANEE IS VERY WEAK NOW!

AND SO SHE MUST REMAIN!
PLAY NICELY WITH YOUR...FRIEND. AND TRY NOT TO MAKE HER **ANGRY**!

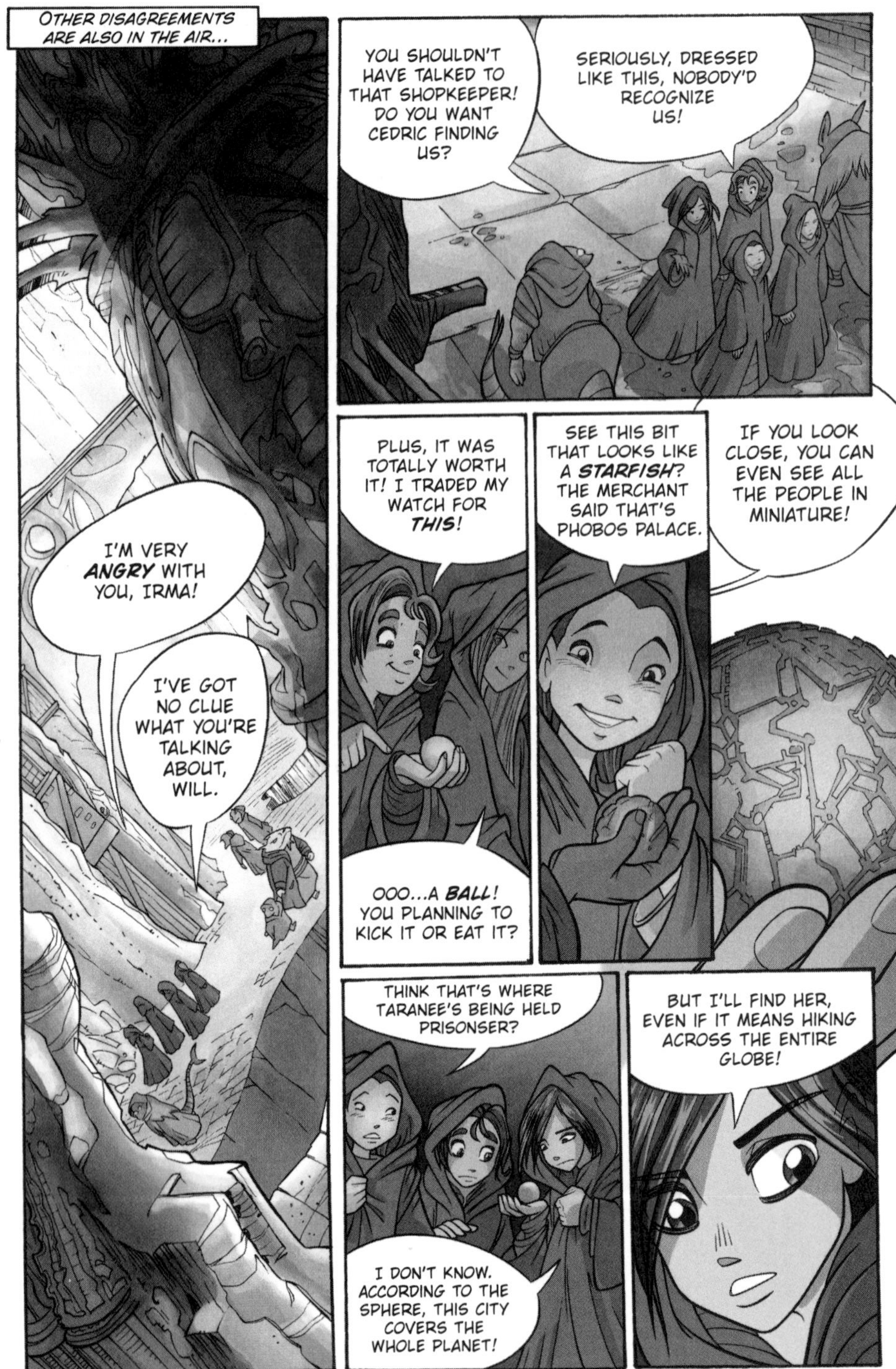
OTHER DISAGREEMENTS ARE ALSO IN THE AIR...
I'M VERY ANGRY WITH YOU, IRMA!
I'VE GOT NO CLUE WHAT YOU'RE TALKING ABOUT, WILL.
YOU SHOULDN'T HAVE TALKED TO THAT SHOPKEEPER! DO YOU WANT CEDRIC FINDING US?
SERIOUSLY, DRESSED LIKE THIS, NOBODY'D RECOGNIZE US!
PLUS, IT WAS TOTALLY WORTH IT! I TRADED MY WATCH FOR THIS!
OOO...A BALL! YOU PLANNING TO KICK IT OR EAT IT?
SEE THIS BIT THAT LOOKS LIKE A STARFISH? THE MERCHANT SAID THAT'S PHOBOS PALACE.
IF YOU LOOK CLOSE, YOU CAN EVEN SEE ALL THE PEOPLE IN MINIATURE!
THINK THAT'S WHERE TARANEE'S BEING HELD PRISONSER?
I DON'T KNOW. ACCORDING TO THE SPHERE, THIS CITY COVERS THE WHOLE PLANET!
BUT I'LL FIND HER, EVEN IF IT MEANS HIKING ACROSS THE ENTIRE GLOBE!

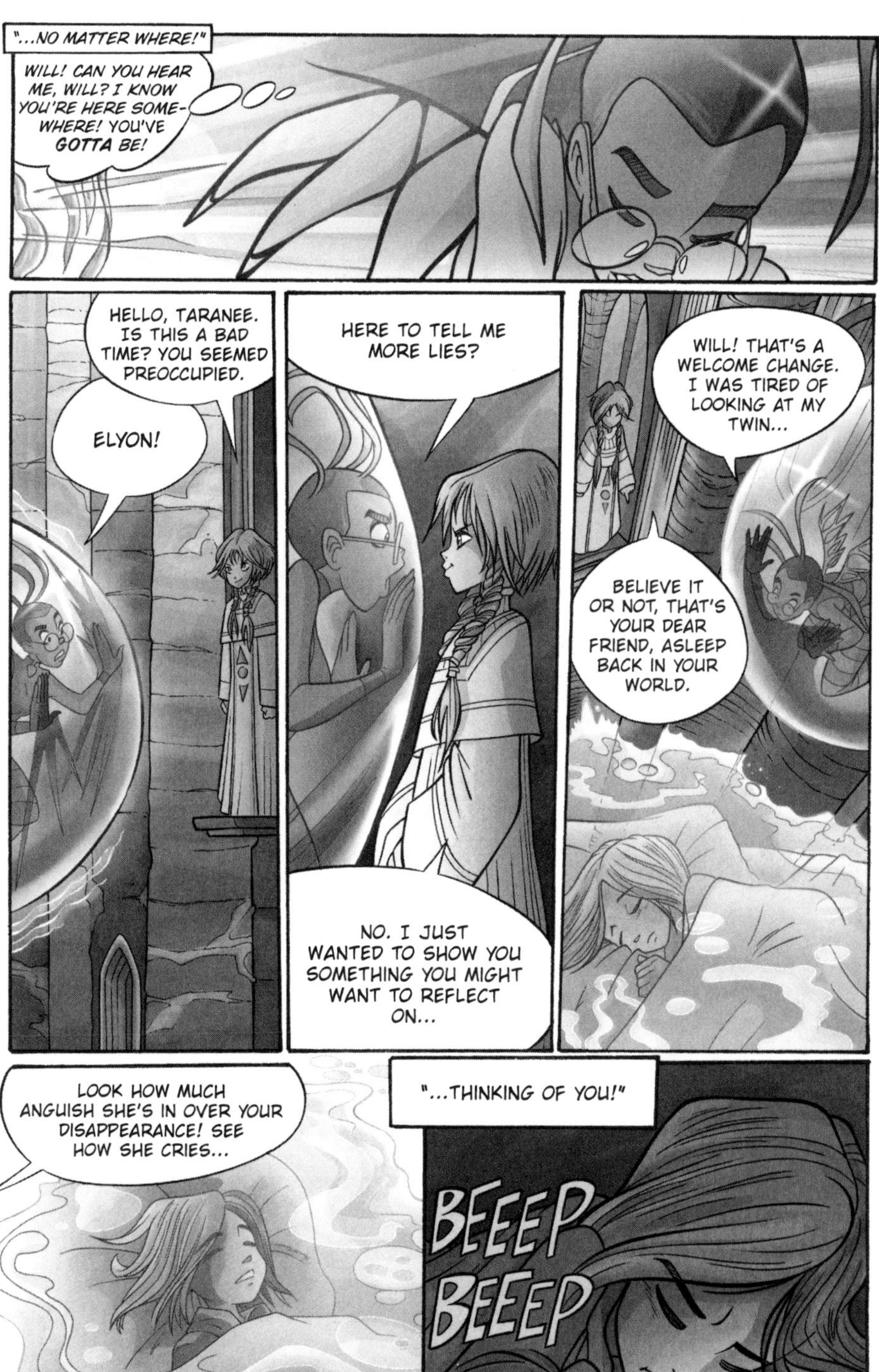
"...NO MATTER WHERE!"
WILL! CAN YOU HEAR ME, WILL? I KNOW YOU'RE HERE SOME-WHERE! YOU'VE GOTTA BE!
HELLO, TARANEE. IS THIS A BAD TIME? YOU SEEMED PREOCCUPIED.
ELYON!
HERE TO TELL ME MORE LIES?
NO. I JUST WANTED TO SHOW YOU SOMETHING YOU MIGHT WANT TO REFLECT ON...
WILL! THAT'S A WELCOME CHANGE. I WAS TIRED OF LOOKING AT MY TWIN...
BELIEVE IT OR NOT, THAT'S YOUR DEAR FRIEND, ASLEEP BACK IN YOUR WORLD.
LOOK HOW MUCH ANGUISH SHE'S IN OVER YOUR DISAPPEARANCE! SEE HOW SHE CRIES...
"...THINKING OF YOU!"
BEEEP
BEEEP

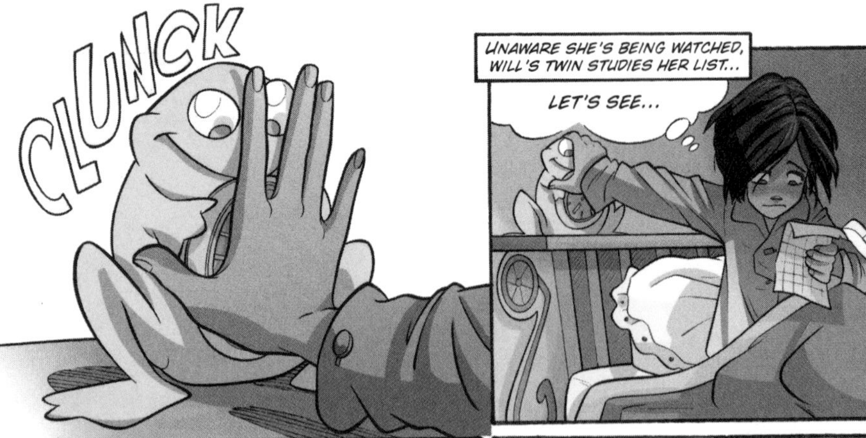
CLUNCK
UNAWARE SHE'S BEING WATCHED, WILL'S TWIN STUDIES HER LIST...
LET'S SEE...

NO! THERE AREN'T ANY INSTRUCTIONS ABOUT A "BEEP"! GOOD NIGHT!

WAIT! AAAH! SEVEN?!

SEVEN! SEVEN! WHAT DOES REAL WILL DO AT SEVEN?

AH! SHE GETS UP!

AH-CHOO!
YES, THAT'S RIGHT, AMANDA...

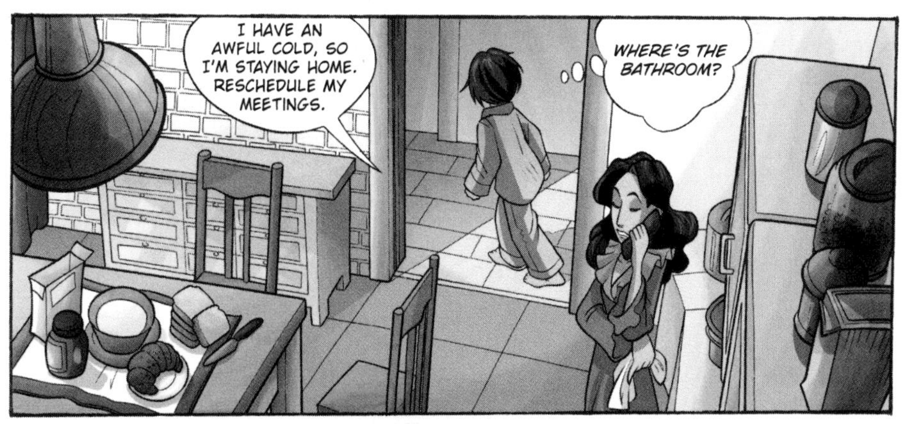
I HAVE AN AWFUL COLD, SO I'M STAYING HOME. RESCHEDULE MY MEETINGS.
WHERE'S THE BATHROOM?

TELL SPENCER TO CHECK THE PRINTOUTS AND...WILL! WHY ARE YOU STILL IN YOUR PAJAMAS?
UH? ARE YOU MY MOTHER?

THEY'RE IN CHARGE OF THE LAYOFFS UNTIL...
...NO, AMANDA, I DON'T MEAN YOU...
BETTER TURN BACK!

WHAT'D I DO WRONG? WHERE'S THAT PAPER?

ARGH! I LOST IT!

THINK! AT 7:00, WAKE UP! QUARTER PAST 7:00— SHOWER! AT TEN TO 8:00, KISS...
KISS...? KISS WHO?

"MAYBE SOME BOY?"
COME ON, DORMOUSE! I KNOW IT HASN'T BEEN LONG, BUT YOU KEPT MY PARENTS UP ALL NIGHT!

IT'S THEIR FAULT I HAVE TO GIVE YOU BACK SO SOON, AND YOUR MASTER OWES ME AN EXPLANA-TION...
DING DONG

WILL! OPEN THE... AH-CHOO!
YEAH, YEAH... HOW DO YOU CLOSE THIS THING?

UH? W-WILL?
MORE OR LESS. WHAT DO YOU WANT?

I'M BRINGING YOUR DORMOUSE BACK. I KNOW IT'S ONLY... AHEM ...7:50, AND YOU...
SEVEN-WHAT NOW? OH YEAH!

THANKS FOR THE REMINDER!
?

AND THANKS FOR THE DORMOUSE TOO...
SLAM
...WHOEVER YOU ARE!

WHEN I GOT HOME YESTERDAY, YOU WERE ALREADY IN BED. I'M STAYING HOME TODAY. ARE YOU HAPPY?
NO, MOM.

AM I TALKING TO THE SAME WILL WHO COMPLAINS I WORK TOO MUCH?
YES, MOM! IS THAT BETTER?
HEY! STOP!

THE PAPER! THAT'S WHERE IT WAS!

WHOOPS! AT TEN TO EIGHT, I WAS S'POSED TO KISS MOM, NOT THAT BOY!
OH NO! ONE OF THE SHOULDN'T DO'S WAS "DON'T KISS ANY BOYS!"

MOOOM! HAVE YOU EVER BEEN KISSED BY MISTAKE?
WHAT A QUESTION! NO! SOME MISTAKES GET REPAID IN SLAPS!

WILL! **WILL!** WOULD YOU STOP FOR A SECOND? I NEED TO TELL YOU SOMETHING!
NOT NOW, MOM! I HAVE TO RESPECT MY **SCHEDULE!**

YOU HAVE A SCHEDULE? THE GIRL WHO NEEDS A CANNON TO WAKE UP?
DO THESE CANNONS GO "BEEP BEEP"?

LET ME DO THAT... I KNOW YOU'LL BE HOME LATER, BUT JUST SO YOU KNOW, I INVITED A **GUEST** FOR DINNER.
OH YEAH...? HEY, IS THAT MY CROISSANT?

THE POINT IS...IT'S **MR. COLLINS!**
MMMPH! **SHO WHAT?**

231

MAYBE I WASN'T CLEAR...I'M TALKING ABOUT **THE** MR. COLLINS!
AWESOME! **HAVE FUN!**

H-HAVE FUN?

SPLASH
WILL KISSED MATT! AND YOU ALWAYS LIKED HIM!
THAT'S ENOUGH, SO SHUT UP!
WHY'D YOU STOP?
I HAVE MY REASONS! YOU THINK ABOUT WHAT YOU SAW! YOU'LL HAVE PLENTY OF TIME IN THERE!
ELYON GOT MAD! THAT MEANS WHAT I SAW IS TRUE!
WILL GOT WHAT YOU ALWAYS DREAMED ABOUT! ARE YOU JEALOUS?
N-NO! I'M LOYAL TO YOU, CEDRIC!
GOOD, BUT KNOW THAT WAS NOT THE REAL WILL! SHE IS HERE—IN MERIDIAN—AND I WILL CATCH HER FOR YOU...

232

"...AT ANY COST."

AH! IT'S HER!

IT'S A DEAD END!
WILL!
LISTEN! THEY'RE COMING!
A STAIRCASE ENDING AT A WALL?! HOW'S THAT EVEN POSSIBLE?
ANYTHING'S POSSIBLE IN MERIDIAN!
?
YOU HAVE NO CHOICE! ENTER THE SHADOW! NOW!
I SAW THEM! THEY WENT DOWN HERE, AND...
HUH?

"WHERE'D THEY GO?"
I CAN'T BELIEVE IT! WE ARE IN A... SHADOW?
FORGET THE LAWS OF PHYSICS THAT RULE YOUR WORLD, IRMA!
HOW DO YOU KNOW MY NAME?
THAT VOICE...
MS. RUDOLPH?
YOU FORCED ME TO ABANDON EARTH, BUT YOU STILL ARE MY STUDENTS.
YOU MOVE WELL IN THE DARK...IS THIS WHERE YOU LIVE NOW?
I WON'T HURT YOU—THOUGH I SHOULD BE ANGRY WITH YOU!
THIS ISN'T JUST THE DARK... THIS IS THE IMMENSE UNDERBELLY OF THE INFINITE CITY!

SO YOU WERE HIDING IN OUR WORLD TOO? FROM WHAT?
A DARK SHROUD COVERS THE SKY AND THE HEARTS OF MY PEOPLE!
BILLIONS OF ANGRY BLACK HEARTS, SAD AND DESPERATE! THIS IS MERIDIAN!
THIS IS DARKNESS!
MY LORD, IF YOU FIND THAT SWINDLER...
YOU HAVE NO CLAIM TO HER, FOOL! YOU WOULD BE WISE TO DISAPPEAR!
FTOOOM
IT'S VERY TOUGH, LORD CEDRIC!
TRY AGAIN, VATHEK! THE ONLY THING BETWEEN US AND THE GUARDIANS IS THIS SHADOW THRESHOLD!
THEY RETURNED TO METAMOOR JUST TO FREE THEIR FRIEND.
YES! TOO BAD THEY'LL NEVER LEAVE!
THAT DOESN'T SOUND GOOD... WHAT DO WE DO?
YOU MUST MAKE A CHOICE. EVEN TIME HAS ITS OWN RULES HERE!
FTOOOM

WHAT DO YOU MEAN?
IN THE CAGE THAT IS MERIDIAN, TIME PASSES MUCH MORE *SLOWLY*!

HOW LONG'S ONE EARTH DAY IN *PRISON* TIME?
ONE, PERHAPS EVEN *TWO WEEKS*!

TARANEE! I LEFT HER IN THE HANDS OF THOSE MONSTERS THAT LONG?
DON'T BLAME YOURSELF! YOU COULDN'T HAVE KNOWN...

AND YOU? HOW DO YOU KNOW WHY WE'RE HERE? WHO ARE YOU, *REALLY*?
TODAY'S LESSON IS OVER, GIRLS!

THERE'S THE BELL...
FTOOOM

DONE! I OPENED A GAP!
WELL DONE, VATHEK! NOW WE HAVE BUT TO FIND THEM, AND...

DON'T WEAR YOURSELF OUT, SNAKE!
YOU?

YES! HERE ARE YOUR CAGES, GUARDIANS! AH-HA-HA!
WE GOT NOTHING TO SAY TO YOU, SO IF YOU'RE GONNA DO SOMETHING, GET IT OVER WITH!
WHY? WHY ALLOW THEMSELVES TO BE CAPTURED?
THIS CITY IS IMMENSE, AND THEY CHOSE THE FASTEST WAY TO BE REUNITED WITH TARANEE!
AM I RIGHT, LITTLE ONE? I SHALL GRANT YOUR WISH, AND YOU WILL GIVE ME THE HEART OF KANDRAKAR!
FIRST, THOUGH, THERE IS SOMEONE WHO WANTS TO SEE YOU PERSONALLY!
WHAT'S HAPPENING? WHERE ARE YOU TAKING US?
NOWHERE. YOU ARE FORBIDDEN IN THE PLACE YOU ARE ABOUT TO SEE! THIS IS MERELY A PROJECTION...

...OF THE GARDEN OF PHOBOS!

IT'S... IT'S...
IT IS USELESS TO ATTEMPT TO ARTICULATE! EVERYTHING HERE IS INSPIRED BY PERFECTION!

IF IT'S SO PERFECT, THEN WHY AM I SCARED?
PERHAPS BECAUSE EVERYTHING YOU SEE IS LETHAL! NOW, QUIET! THEY ARE HERE!

THE MURMURERS! PHOBOS'S COURT! VOICE AND EYES OF THE PRINCE OF PRINCES!
...youguardians...

...youguardians...
...earthlyguardians earthly...
...guardiansyoudon't...

...earthearthly guar...
THEIR VOICES ARE LIKE WHISPERS! ALMOST THOUGHTS!
WHAT YOU SEE DIMS YOUR OTHER SENSES. CLOSE YOUR EYES AND LISTEN!

you, guardians of earth.
unworthy to approach us.
May your end be favorable.
And may the oracle learn...
...to respect us.

I DON'T UNDER-STAND!
IT'S NOT IMPORTANT! WHAT'S IMPORTANT IS THAT THEY HAVE SEEN YOU!

WHERE ARE THEY GOING NOW?
THAT DOESN'T CONCERN YOU EITHER! THE TIME HAS COME FOR YOU TO KNOW...

"...THE MERIDIAN PRISON..."

WHAT A DUMP! BET YOU NEVER BROUGHT YOUR PRETTY FRIENDS HERE!
THEY ARE NOT MADE TO LIVE IN MERIDIAN. THE SCUM LIVE BEYOND THE CASTLE OF PHOBOS!
AND YOU, CEDRIC? WHERE DO YOU BELONG?
HERE, FOR NOW, BUT MUCH DEPENDS ON YOU. SPARE YOURSELF SUFFERING. GIVE ME THE HEART OF KANDRAKAR!
FORGET IT!
WRONG ANSWER, WILL.
TARANEE!
YES, IT'S HER.
ELYON! YOU MUSTN'T BRING HER HERE! I GAVE YOU EXPLICIT ORDERS!
BUT I COULDN'T MISS THIS. WATCH!
TARANEE! TALK TO US! ARE YOU OKAY?
TARANEE, DON'T YOU RECOGNIZE US?
QUIET! I DON'T WANT TO LISTEN TO YOU!

YOU'RE JUST ILLUSIONS! FRAUDS! I'M SICK OF YOU! GO AWAY! **GO!**

BUT TARANEE, WE...

ENOUGH ***TRICKS***! I'LL DO ANYTHING YOU WANT! JUST TAKE ME FAR AWAY FROM HERE...***NOW!***

HEAR THAT, WILL? WHEN I'M THROUGH WITH YOU, YOU'LL KNEEL AND GIVE ME WHAT I WANT!

YOU'LL PAY FOR THIS, ELYON!

AND YOU'LL ROT IN THIS PRISON! YOU'LL ***NEVER*** KISS MATT!

IF THAT'S WHAT YOU'RE WORRIED ABOUT, YOU CAN RELAX!

BUT I...
I SAW YOU!
?
?

MATT? I SAW YOU KISSING HIM!
WHAT? NO, I NEVER DID THAT!
ENOUGH, ELYON! TAKE HER AWAY!

IT WAS ONE OF ELYON'S TRICKS...OR MAYBE YOU SAW MY **TWIN** ON EARTH?
DO AS I SAY! NOW!

IT DIDN'T HAPPEN! **READ MY MIND** IF YOU DON'T BELIEVE ME!
TARANEE! SHE'S LY—

SHE'S TELLING THE TRUTH!

ONLY THE REAL WILL WOULD KNOW I'M **TELEPATHIC!**
YOU...YOU JUST TOYED WITH MY EMOTIONS! BUT NO ONE SHOULD PLAY...
...WITH FIRE!
WHOOOOSH

SHE'S... SHE'S MELTING THE CAGE!
I TOLD YOU NOT TO MAKE HER ANGRY!
WHOOSSH
SHE DIDN'T SPEND ENOUGH TIME IN THE CAGE TO BE STRIPPED OF HER VITAL ENERGY!
C-CEDRIC! DO SOMETHING!
I CAN'T! THE POWER OF FIRE IS THE MOST INDOMITABLE OF ALL! RUN! RUN!
KRAAAAAM
KRAAAAM
NO, TARANEE! STOP!

WILL, I HAVE TO...
YOU HAVE TO TRUST ME!

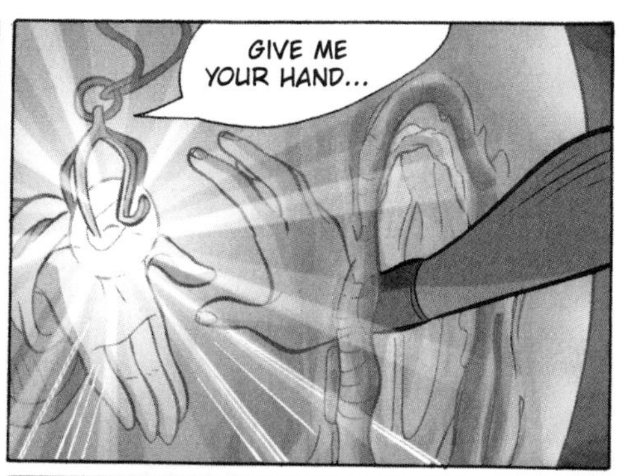
GIVE ME YOUR HAND...

THERE... NOW I'M POWERLESS TO STOP THEM!

CEDRIC! ELYON! THEY'RE GETTING AWAY!
LET THEM GO, HAY LIN. THEY KNOW THE TRAPS IN THIS WORLD TOO WELL.
AS FOR US, IT'S TIME TO GO HOME!
TOO BAD! WE TRANSFORMED FOR NOTHING!
NOT FOR NOTHING! IT'S A SALUTE TO OUR REUNION WITH...
...TARANEE!
MEANWHILE, SOMEONE WATCHES...
...FROM KANDRAKAR.
YOU'RE SMILING, ORACLE?
EVENTS HAVE UNBURDENED ME OF THE WEIGHT OF A SERIOUS DECISION, TIBOR!

WHAT PUNISHMENT AWAITS THE GUARDIANS?
NONE. THEY OVERCAME AN IMPORTANT TRIAL, PROVING THAT THEY ARE INDEED THE CHOSEN ONES!
"BUT NOW, SILENCE! WATCH AS THEY RETURN TO THEIR LIVES..."
WELL? HOW DO YOU FEEL?
IT'S...IT'S FANTASTIC! WHEN I MERGED WITH MY ASTRAL DROP, I GOT ALL ITS MEMORIES AND FEELINGS!
IT'S LIKE I WAS NEVER GONE!
OH, TARANEE!
TARANEE! IT'S COLD! DID YOU FIND WHAT YOU NEEDED IN THE GARDEN?
YES, FATHER!
NOW I HAVE EVERYTHING I NEED!

THAT NIGHT...
TRUNCK CLUNK
IRMA!
MOM! YOU'RE STILL UP?
WHAT ABOUT YOU? DIDN'T I SEE YOU GO TO YOUR ROOM EARLIER?
ERR... YOU'RE RIGHT! ACTUALLY, I'M GOING BACK RIGHT NOW!
NIGHT, THEN! I JUST WANTED TO SAY HOW KIND YOU'VE BEEN LATELY.
KIND HOW...?
AGREEING TO GO ON A DATE WITH THAT BOY, THE ONE YOU TURNED DOWN YESTERDAY. WHAT'S HIS NAME...?
THE SHOUT "MARTIN!" ECHOES ALL THE WAY TO WILL'S HOUSE.
YEAH, DORMOUSE! I HEARD IT TOO. IF HER HOUSE WASN'T SO FAR, I'D SWEAR THAT WAS IRMA'S VOICE.

NO, I'M NOT MAD...EVEN IF YOU DID PRACTICALLY DISINTEGRATE MY ROOM.
AT LEAST I KNOW WHAT MY ASTRAL DROP FELT WHEN SHE KISSED MATT.
"I JUST WISH SHE HADN'T TRACKED HIM DOWN AT SCHOOL AND SMACKED HIM IN FRONT OF EVERYBODY!"
FUNNY... MY LIFE IS RUINED, BUT THE WORST PART IS...
...MY MOM'S ABOUT TO HAVE DINNER WITH THE MAN I HATE MOST! I DON'T KNOW WHAT TO DO...
WILL! ARE YOU BACK?
CAN YOU COME DOWN HERE FOR A MINUTE?

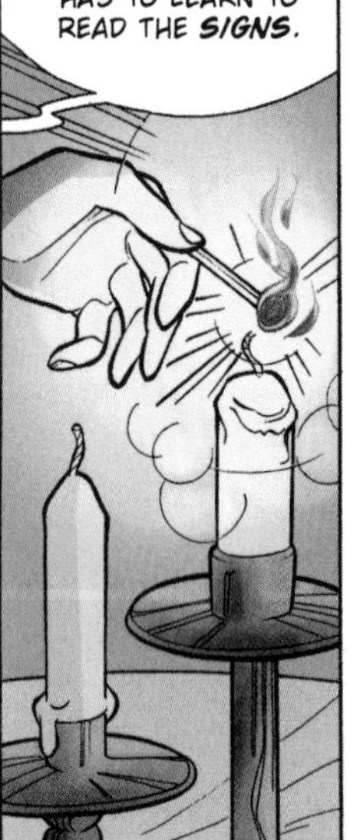

"...BETWEEN FRIENDS..."

END OF CHAPTER 4

Read on in Volume 2!

ASTONISHED BY...

Will

14 years old

Born January 19, Capricorn

5'1" tall

Slightly withdrawn, very sensitive and easily hurt

Her favorite subjects are Biology and Science.

Suffers from seasonal allergies

Loves water sports and her stuffed animal collection

Twirls her hair when embarrassed

Lives with her mother, a consultant at Simultech in an apartment on the outskirts of town

In witch form

Her **wings**, like the other girls (except Hay Lin), are incapable of flight.

Will is the custodian of the Heart of Kandrakar, the jewel housing the secrets of Air, Water, Earth, and Fire. Guarding the strength of the four elements, the jewel multiplies their force in Will's own absolute energy.

Both comfortable and sturdy—not to mention always fashionable!—Will's **boots** keep the most fearsome opponents at bay.

ASTONISHED BY...

Irma

13 years old

Born March 13, Pisces

The most generous of the group, detests all sports but can spend hours and hours listening to her favorite idols

A member of Class 2B at the Sheffield Institute along with Cornelia and Hay Lin

Can direct questioning with the power of her thoughts

Lives in a house with a little garden with her father, who's a policeman; her mother, who stays at home, and her little brother, who has a turtle named Lettuce

In witch form

Controls the power of **water**

Irma is amazingly adept at commanding liquids. She can lounge for hours and hours in water without getting pruney. She's also a killer spellcaster. Woe to those who get on her bad side!

Stargazes with Will and Hay Lin (Full disclosure—she doesn't get along too well with Cornelia, who's too sophisticated for Irma's sense of humor.)

Her sense of **humor** is just as sharp when she's transformed—her quick comebacks are her secret weapon!

Part I. The Twelve Portals • Volume I

Series Created by Elisabetta Gnone
Comic Art Direction: Alessandro Barbucci, Barbara Canepa

JY
1290 Avenue of the Americas
New York, NY 10104

Visit us at yenpress.com
facebook.com/yenpress
twitter.com/yenpress
yenpress.tumblr.com
instagram.com/yenpress

First JY Edition: October 2017

JY is an imprint of Yen Press, LLC.
The JY name and logo are trademarks of Yen Press, LLC.

The publisher is not responsible for websites (or their content) that are not owned by the publisher.

Library of Congress Control Number: 2017950917

ISBNs:
978-0-316-47692-8 (paperback)
978-0-316-41500-2 (ebook)

10 9 8 7 6 5 4 3 2 1

LSC-C

Printed in the United States of America

Cover Art by Alessandro Barbucci
Color and Light Direction by Barbara Canepa
Colors by Mara Damiani

Translation Assistance by Eva Martina Allione
Lettering by Katie Blakeslee

HALLOWEEN

Concept by Elisabetta Gnone
Script by Elisabetta Gnone and Francesco Artibani
Art by Alessandro Barbucci
Color and Light Direction by Barbara Canepa
Inks by Donald Soffritti
Colors by Mara Damiani
Title Page Art by Alessandro Barbucci with Color Direction by Barbara Canepa and Colors by Andrea Cagol

THE TWELVE PORTALS

Concept by Elisabetta Gnone
Script by Francesco Artibani
Layout by Alessandro Barbucci
Pencils by Manuela Razzi
Color and Light Direction by Barbara Canepa
Inks by Roberta Zanotta
Title Page Art by Alessandro Barbucci
with Colors by Barbara Canepa

THE DARK DIMENSION

Concept and Script by Francesco Artibani
Art by Gianluca Paniello and Daniela Vetro
Inks by Marina Baggio and Donald Soffritti
Color and Light Direction by Barbara Canepa
Title Page Art by Alessandro Barbucci and Barbara Canepa
with Colors by Mara Damiani

THE POWER OF FIRE

Concept and Script by Bruno Enna
Art by Graziano Barbaro
Inks by Marina Baggio and Roberta Zanotta
Color and Light Direction by Barbara Canepa
Title Page Art by Alessandro Barbucci with Colors by Barbara Canepa and Mara Damiani